the cats of benares

GERALDINE HALLS

the cats of ❀ BENARES

Harper & Row, Publishers ✿ *New York and Evanston*

FIRST U.S. EDITION

LIBRARY OF CONGRESS CATALOG CARD NUMBER: 67-22515

H-R

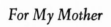

For My Mother

the cats of benares

Prologue

RICHARD WAS IN BENARES THEN, ON ONE OF THOSE VAGUE, ONE-man missions for collecting facts that we already know. . . . A quick dash around the schools in the United Provinces and a hundred thousand words on what needs to be done for rural education.

He took a room in a nice, old-fashioned hotel. And he had his wife with him. Sensitive, pretty thing. You know the sort of woman—touch her with a feather and up comes a big black bruise. Imagine what Benares can do to a disposition like that. And, needless to say, dear Pamela has never learnt her limitations, for in no time at all off they went to look at Siva's temple.

In case you've never been there, let me tell you about that salubrious spot. First you go through a bazaar of more than usual character. Filth, flies, beggars . . . whole, sick and holy. This is Benares, remember, that remarkable city. Then the road gets very narrow and if you're driving a car—which, sensibly, they were—you have to stop. And then the touts descend, like kites on a dead dog.

You fight that battle, and one tout wins, leading you down a delectable lane. No sun falls into it. It is so narrow that by stretching out your arms you could touch the walls on either side—except that it wouldn't occur to you to want to touch anything. Discarded marigold garlands have been trodden under foot and pulped into thick yellow mud. You slush along and a million flies lift up and cover you. To keep them out of your mouth, you gulp for breath into your handkerchief. You have seen something of India—you must have seen something to have got so far—but you feel now that you are walking down the hollow center of a bone, the one bone in the Indian anatomy that is most centrally placed.

You pass old ladies squatting in a row and holding out their begging bowls. They have come to this filthy, fly-infested spot to die—but why should you be shocked? For them to be here is the sure guarantee of salvation, and their happiness shows in their gaunt, collapsed faces. But their physical degradation is so totally unacceptable to you, you refuse to see their joy. Instead, you ask yourself what—with such an introduction—can be waiting for you there at the end of the lane where the roof of the temple shines (gold, no less) and the heaps of rotting flowers sicken the air.

Richard and Pamela never got so far. Suddenly she stopped and gripped his sleeve. "I'm sorry," she said. "I'm *sorry!* I can't go on!"

She turned and, her feet slipping in the marigold mud, she ran, and the touts ran after her, shouting, "Memsahib! Memsahib!" A word which, in any case, she detested, belonging, as it does, to the bad old days. Little boys ran too and lepers came. They thrust their crumbling fingers in her face and it seemed to her that all the misery and importunity of India would seize her and pull her down. She felt them snatching her eyes, to put where they had none. She felt their hands in her belly, scooping her entrails out so that they could eat up what remained of her dinner. When Richard reached the car she was crouched within, trembling with revulsion and terror.

For days after that she refused to leave the hotel. She read Gandhi's autobiography, and then she read Nehru's. She liked Nehru's better; he thought like a European, in her view. Then she got bored, and boredom drove her out into some of the nicer, cleaner parts of the town. But always in a car, insulated, as it were, against—against what? Leprosy isn't infectious, is it? Against other people's misery, I suppose. You know how it is here.

To live in India you must have an enormous heart. Or no heart at all. That's the best answer of course if you want to survive. It's the in-betweens that have the tough time. Like Pamela. The lepers and the old ladies had been too much for her. She couldn't run the risk of having to look at them again, but at the same time she couldn't help being aware that they were there on the other side of the hotel's long, high wall, kept out by that beturbaned chaukidar. Lepers and old ladies, dirt, sores and intentionally multilated children. No suttee, alas! The good old days have gone.

The hotel where Pamela and Richard were staying contained an immense population of half-starved stray cats. Two hundred and forty-six to be exact: figures arrived at by a United Nations sociologist who took a cat census about that time. He had time on his hands, his counterpart having effectively blocked the more ambitious project laid down in his program of work. Some of the cats were quite beautiful, having in their remoter ancestry noble Persian blood. Others had lost eyes and limbs when in kittenhood they struggled to survive. Occasionally the hotel staff tried to get rid of them by collecting all they could in bags and dumping them in the fish market—whether there to be fed or skinned and filleted I do not know. They invariably found their way back again, accompanied by other fish-market cats with whom they had formed amorous connections.

The bearers, being gentle Hindus with a holy respect for the God-given gift of life, would not destroy them, though they did, on one occasion, shut up some fifty or more in an unoccupied room, leaving them there without food or water and hoping that God might take a hand. You know what flexible minds Indians have. But God wasn't given a chance. Some indignant European —and aren't we Europeans forever interfering in God's purposes?—heard their cries and let them out.

It was a heart-rending spectacle. Out they tottered into the sunlight—thin, starved, almost too weak to walk. That furry and undefeatable army; another army of hopeful kites knitting the air above them.

Pamela happened to witness the scene and, snatching up a kitten, the prettiest, took it back to her room and gave it a saucer of milk. As it happened, she wasn't a cat lover, she much preferred dogs; but the sight of those suffering animals had moved her, and when next day another kitten turned up at feeding time, she hadn't the heart to send it away.

The newcomer, in fact, wasn't a kitten at all. It was just an undersized cat. And it was pregnant. Well, to cut a long story short, where do you draw the line? That pregnant one produced its litter of six, and, mother by now being strong and well fed, all six survived. Pamela kept them. Richard was away at the time, and she herself was far too squeamish to wring their necks or drop them in a bucket of water. And of course the bearers would never take life, except by that gentle Indian method of slow starvation. She gave some away. The chaukidar took one, but when it grew up and lost its looks he stopped feeding it, so it found its way back again. In the meantime other cats had heard of the welfare service and came for food or abandoned their kittens on her doorstep. She ended up, believe it or not, with thirty-eight cats. A nice credible figure, don't you think? That room—and I'm not exaggerating, I saw it—was a kind of Bosch nightmare. Cats everywhere. If you sat down there'd be one under the cushion. If you opened a drawer another would fly out at you. They were on the bookcase, in the wastepaper basket, under the bed. The place stank of cooking and of sexual intercourse and the noise was horrible. Pamela sat in the middle of all this with a kind of blank look on her face. The whole thing was really getting out of hand.

And what did Richard have to say about it all? Well, his job took him out a good deal. He did a lot of traveling. Sometimes he was away from Benares a week at a time. His domestic life was not exactly harmonious, and when the first kittens came he was rather pleased. Some little playmates, he thought, might do her good. Even five or six kittens didn't alarm him. It was a relief to find her talking obsessively about cats instead of going on and on about the heat, the stupidity of the bearers, the brutality of the management, the rotten food and her inability to sleep.

Time passed and the cat population began to build up but, as with all things that happen under our eyes, he barely noticed. Then he went away again, to Calcutta this time. There was a girl—and he remained away rather longer than duty required.

When he got back he was told that his presence in the U.P. was no longer wanted. He was being transferred to a project in New Delhi. He was glad. There was something of the adventurer in him and what was new was always promising. But in his hotel that night the scales fell from his eyes.

There was his wife in their room with the dirty saucers, the chopped-up meat, the ants hauling fish bones over the floor; and thirty-eight cats, three of which were on the way to producing again.

"You've got to do something," he said.

"But what?" she asked. And outside in the night yet more starving and destitute cats clamored for charity.

"It's got to stop."

"What can I do? Help me!"

It was an old familiar refrain and it made him angry. "You're always getting yourself into messes," he said, "and then expecting someone else to get you out of them. We're leaving for Delhi in two weeks' time. What are you going to do then? You can't take them with you. You'll have to abandon them. Do you think you've helped them? That army of brutes out there will eat them alive."

She looked about at her protégés. Fat, happy cats curled up in cushions, purring and licking their paws. She began to cry.

"What you've done," he told her, "is stupid, sentimental and self-indulgent. The only thing that's better off is your conscience. You've simply deprived these creatures of the power to survive."

Well, you couldn't blame him. And he didn't mean that he wouldn't help her. He was just fed up. On top of all those unwanted feline dependents, there was this girl in Calcutta.

Silence fell, between man and wife, that is. The cats did not observe it. And the next day he went away on yet another trip, but without a goodbye kiss or a tender word. He swears, however—and who can prove otherwise?—that he lay awake that night devising a plan. On the following Sunday he would take Pamela out all day, and during their absence a vet would go to their room and painlessly dispose of all that lived there. He moreover declares that she knew she could count on him. She had always counted on him in the past, and he had never failed her. But perhaps his words stung her pride.

Next morning, after he had gone, she rang up the Government vet. He came in the afternoon, bringing with him a sack and a long, blunt syringe. An Indian, and a Hindu too, but don't let that surprise you. Nobody in India holds any but extreme opinions, and it was the vet's belief that all unproductive creatures should be exterminated. What did cats do? They sewed not, neither did they spin. They simply ate. And India, in its present economic state, could not afford to support them. Or monkeys or peacocks, or squirrels, or old cows. Or beggars? Or lepers? Or sick old men?

He tackled his job with zeal, but animals have a sensitive nose for death, and by the time the first little pussy lay prone, the others were backing away, saliva dripping from their jaws. Then they were flying around the room all claws and fur and letting out bloodcurdling screams that rang through the hotel, so that all those life-loving bearers quickly got to know what murderous acts were being done within. My God! What a holocaust! The

vet put on long rubber gloves and a mask on his face. He took
the sheets off the beds and flung them about to trap the flying
kittens. It took all the afternoon. The chairs broke, the covers
were in strips; the room stank of terror.

And Pamela? She watched the whole thing. Wholesale
slaughter at her own decree. It takes a lot of nerve, and Hitler, as
far as we know, never had to sit and watch.

Neither, for that matter, did Pamela, but watch she did. And
I wonder why. I often think about it. I know them both, and the
question intrigues me. Proving herself before Richard, do you
suppose? Or cooking up a little slow revenge.

When he came back the vet had gone and there she was quite
normal and calm. But no bearer or sweeper would go within
yards of her room. They went about muttering and looking at
her out of the sides of their eyes. They wouldn't serve her in the
dining room. Richard had to take her food in on a tray. When
she went out into the streets small boys threw stones. All Benares
—that holy city—knew that she was bad luck.

She held up through it all with admirable fortitude, nursing
her crack-up carefully and lovingly within her. Sometimes the
weak can be awfully strong, haven't you noticed? It took a whole
twelve months to bring her down. And I suppose there must
have been a last straw. But it was something quite unimportant
and small, so small nobody even knows what it was. Not even
Richard, or if he does he won't say. They were in Delhi then—
he came back from work one day to find her . . . well . . .
nobody quite knows. So then he put her on a plane and flew her
home.

Chapter One

THE MONSOON WAS ALMOST OVER, AND THE LAWN WAS A SPONGY
sward, with the angular shadow of the hotel roof beginning to
push the sunlight back across it. On the long veranda Nur, the
sweeper, squatted, his naked legs—the stringy, fleshless legs of
India's debased classes—bent up like hairpins as he shuffled
along like a crab, drawing with his greasy rag slow half-circular
patterns in a six-hour deposit of New Delhi dust.

I broke off a piece of cake and crumbled it for the sparrows.
Adominable cake, tasting of lemon essence and egg powder. I
hadn't been able to eat it four months ago and it was no better
now, but it was an element in a scene toward which I felt an
undiscriminating affection.

Overhead, high up in the sun-filled sky, cattle egret flew in
precise formation—the tip of a huge white arrow that would fall
and break apart somewhere in the waterlogged fields off the Agra
road. It was the time for birds and, flying lower down, just over
the tops of the trees, crows were coming in to their night roosts

in the Delhi gardens. Hoopoes strutted on the lawn like clock-work toys. They were very tame and hardly bothered to get out of the way when a woman approached from the other side of the garden, crossed the red gravel drive and walked on the grass.

Young—around thirty, I thought, as I watched her; for thirty looks very young from my forty-second year. Tall, slight, with a small sharp-cut face and short, bright hair. She had extremely long legs, abnormally long from the knee to the groin, so that when she bent down to take off her sandals and continued walking on barefoot, she didn't look heavy and truncated, as most women do without their shoes, but lithe and light, tipped forward a little and springing from the balls of her feet.

Why do we see beauty in one human being and not in another? Beauty, I mean, that is like a personal message, and leaves the rest of the world unconcerned. Is it an ingredient absent from our diet for which our constitution hungers? The antidote to whatever has caused us suffering, the sudden relief from a long deficiency? And if so, then is love a time and a place? I have often asked myself these questions.

Now she had come to the edge of the veranda and, sitting down, she put her sandals on again; crossing first one leg, then the other; bending with a straight back to pull the shoes on her brown, narrow feet. Her little scene was over and there had been nothing very remarkable about it, yet I found myself moved, as though I had been watching actions of exceptional charm—movements of certainty and freshness that seemed to use all her faculties, that were not mechanical but experienced and in-tended. The message her brain sent to her body was so clear and unconditional I could read it for myself, so that just to watch her was to share her sensual life. No doubt or embarrassment, no last-minute attack of fear, no pause for the permission of the world. The very shining summit of sanity.

"Ah, Mr. Mardellis! Mr. Mardellis!" called Soni, coming toward me with hands outstretched.

Soni was the owner of the hotel, and it was Prasad who had told me how he happened to acquire it.

"Mr. Soni," he said, "came from Lahore at the time of the massacres. They crept out at night with just what food there was in the house and a few rupees. His brother would not leave and the Moslems butchered him. When the river floods its banks, who can restrain it? Indian Government gave him that house in compensation for the loss of his property. It belonged to a Moslem, a judge in the I.C.S., but that man had gone to Pakistan. Mr. Soni started with nothing, just a house and a hundred rupees. Now he is worth crores. He is one of the wealthiest men in Delhi."

There was no note of condemnation in Prasad's voice. He merely offered the tale of this mercurial rise to fortune for my interest and wonderment. Then he said, "At that time Mr. Soni always wore khadi and a Gandhi cap. Now he wears imported English cloth and no hat at all. Except for public functions."

This prompted me to say that someone had told me not to trust an Indian in a Gandhi cap. He was always up to something. But you can never push Prasad. He slides out of your way just when you think you've maneuvered him into position. "We must trust one another," he said. "Where would we be without trust?"

I hadn't seen Soni since my return so I had to shake his soft damp hand, and talk.

How was England? How was my wife? Ah, she had stayed in London. He offered me a long pitying glance.

Soni was a small man, and fanatically gentle. He held his body at less than its height as though to accentuate his nature's humility, and when he told me, as he did now, that his wife, Lakshmi, was visiting her daughter in Bombay and that, like me, he was all alone, he made it sound as though this was a deserved penance that life had put upon him. I commiserated. Then it turned out that he wasn't alone at all, for another daughter was visiting him from Calcutta and had brought all her beautiful children with her.

We looked at three little girls who were dashing about on the lawn with a big red ball. Plaits swinging like black ropes, long flowered sherwanis and dopattas floating.

"They are my granddaughters," he whispered devotedly. "You have no children, Mr. Mardellis?"

"No children," I said firmly, declining to be overpowered by this misfortune.

But Soni clasped his hands and smiled at me with all the condescension of the richly endowed. "Ah! Mr. Mardellis, children are our blessings. They are the flowers of life."

I knew already of his devotion to little ones, as I knew of his passion for birds and flowers, which was part and parcel of his adoration of God, his oneness with the universe. It was only money that he didn't care about. His was a thick, opaque presence, sweet to taste, sticky to touch, and by the time I had prized myself from it, my girl of the long legs was walking away.

All as before.

A thin, sick yellow light. A brown stain around the wall, about five feet four inches from the floor, where a succession of bearers had leaned their oiled heads. Big clicking fans that cooled the tinted soup.

The swing door leading to the kitchens shrieked like a wounded kitten as the bearers crashed back and forth. Mice ran about on the floor. Sometimes, when their numbers became too abundant, the bearers would catch them in tablecloths or painless traps, carry them tenderly outside and let them loose in the garden. Here a few might fall to the crows and kites, but the majority found their way back again. Mice and men—there was room for both in this tender and brutal country.

Alisulman. A neat little Moslem with a carefully trimmed, patent black mustache and enormous eyes, stupid with sickness and resignation. Like most of India, he was wearing someone else's clothes, and his uniform had been made for a much larger man. His trousers sank into pools around his naked feet and his sleeves hung down over his hands, hiding them from view, so that he seemed not to have any. He gave me the menu, stood waiting at my side and went to sleep for a moment or two. Being underfed and sick with recurring bouts of dysentery, he was always tired. But never having experienced good health, he did not know what it was and innocently assumed that he enjoyed it. His condition was the common lot; India is full of people who, if they only knew it, ought to be dying.

"I see we've still got mice, Alisulman."

His eyes lit up and he smiled. He loved me that day, as all Indians love anyone who returns. "Tika, Sahib! Plenty mice."

"And the door still squeaks."

"No sir, is oiled."

And all that was not as before.

Myself . . . complete, contained, directing an existence surprisingly my own, without reference to any other human being. So that my mind rejected all the undeniable shortcomings: the gray, gluey bread, the smell on the table linen of dirty dhobi tanks. And my body rejoiced, having cast off two layers of clothing, so that the September air—thick, damp, the steam-bath breath of the monsoon—pawed it with a palpable, animal touch.

The shortest distance between two points is a straight line. Point A to B. And the best route to follow, providing you are not required to feel your way through the swamps and thickets of another's nature, emerging muddy, scratched, your judgments dazed and your heart brimmed with deceptions that are not your own. Yet it seems that we can only escape one captivity to seek another, and I certainly, perhaps more than most, am incapable of living alone. Half alive, leaving unused my powers to love and oppress. A broken watch, counting the minutes but not the hours. Part of time, but neglected by eternity.

At a table not far from my own sat a man, stooped in his chair, his round, soft, womanish shoulders curved over a scooped-out chest. Dark, with black hair growing in a pronounced peak very low on a furrowed brow. Not bad-looking; I suppose you might have called it a thoughtful, sensitive face, though at the time I didn't take to it much. Catching my eye, he smiled, and under that narrow, lined, anxious brow the sun broke out in a glare of big white teeth.

He got up and came across to my table. "I do hope you will excuse me for butting in. I am Fred Siegel and I know who you are because I have heard all about you." We shook hands and I told myself that he was around forty, perhaps a little less, but getting soft and slack; a stomach had begun to bulge under his belt.

He said, "I know all about your vork. I am von of the brother-hood."

Brotherhood? Brotherhood! But he was not a Mason or a supporter of Moral Rearmament. A UNESCO expert, it turned out. A geologist, sent out to a new research project that was being started in Rajasthan. And why should he be interested in me? I had a distinct impression that he wanted something.

"My vife and I are Australians. I believe we are fellow countrymen."

More brotherhood! "I'm English," I said.

The big smile went on. "Zey told me in Paris that you were Australian."

So I explained how I had been recruited into UNESCO from Sydney six years ago.

"You were in Sydney six years ago? In '52? But that is *extraordinary!* So was I!" And I had to be told how he had been working then for some Americans who were prospecting for oil.

He sat down. Then got up. Was he disturbing me? Did I mind? Down he sat again. He had only been in New Delhi for two weeks. He was just cutting his new Delhi teeth. He had heard I was coming back and had been looking forward with all his soul to meeting me. "Last week," he said, "we were having dinner with Malcolm Scott. He told me all about your project. He said you have done a vunderful job out here."

Well, he might have a thick Teutonic accent but his use of English wasn't bad. He managed to invest that statement with just the right nuance of meaning. Sir Malcolm Scott was the head of the U.N. Missions—a grave, reserved man with a dis-tinguished career behind him: ex-Indian Civil Service; then after Independence he had been appointed to New York and had headed some conciliatory missions to Syria, to Iraq, to

Kashmir. He was known to be a close personal friend of Nehru. And now Fred Siegel was the close personal friend of Sir Malcolm Scott.

"I would very much like to see your project someday. I believe you have a most impressive audio-visual section. I am interested in photography. I have a Leica and a Rolleiflex. . . ." And off he went on what he had and where it had all come from. Aden, Hong Kong, Singapore. . . . He seemed to have been in every duty-free port and picked up all there was to buy cheaper than anyone else.

I felt I could see the trend of the conversation and the subtle obligations of brotherhood. It was difficult picking up photographic materials in Delhi at that time. They fell under Government import restrictions and what film there was was usually out of date, or exposed film rewound on old cassettes.

He half rose to his feet. "I must not disturb you any longer. I am so pleased to have met you." Again we shook hands. "I hope we shall see a lot of you. I tell you vat. Would you come and have a drink after dinner? I have a bottle of Scotch in my room. Isn't it a terrible price you have to pay for drink? Zey did not tell us in Paris. But this was a gift from a friend who gets it duty free. . . ."

"I'm sorry, but I'm going out."

"Vat about tomorrow then?"

Then I saw her coming through the door, and he slid out of focus as the light picked her up.

In my half-expectant, lazy, adventurous mood I had been watching for her through the evening and now that I saw her again she looked like someone I had known for a long time.

There was that small, precise, rather hard little face, the face of a charming boy; and there again that unseizable quality of life. From the open door she walked across the room, like a chorister singing the praises of heaven. My awful new friend of the glaring smile turned and held out his hand.

"Here is my wife. Darling, this is Dick Mardellis that we have been hearing so much about. And, Dick—you don't mind if I call you Dick, do you?—this is my wife, Helen."

Even that, after the first shock, didn't seem to matter. Like an arrow aimed at the heart, a mortal blow, it fell off the armor of her special gift and left her untouched.

"I don't remember having heard anything in particular about Mr. Mardellis," she said, looking up at me with a smile that was all untempered delight. It was happiness to meet me. But then everything was happiness. Bright, shadowless, high-noon happiness.

"Darling, you *remember*." He put his arm about her and gave her a little shake. "You remember at Malcolm Scott's. He was talking about that Village Project just outside Delhi."

"Was he?" she said, teasing him. "Never mind. I'm sure Mr. Mardellis is awfully nice, even if I don't remember how important he is, and I'm very glad to meet him."

Later he recollected that his dinner was getting cold. I promised to visit them the following night, and then we parted, deserting one another for the joys of oxtail stew.

I swallowed a trembling slab of caramel custard, her naked shoulders and neat little head poised on the edge of my vision. A good-natured, trivial conversation came toward me in fragments. It sounded like the credit side of a ledger: solid assets proving the day well spent. She had bought a piece of silk in the Cottage

Industries Emporium and on the way home had seen three men on camels at India Gate . . . red turbans like bundles of washing, and the camels with their wobbly lips and bracelets of bells clanking under their knees. Farther on she had stopped to look at a tomb, and a man had played weird music on a gourd. Then a mongoose had had a fight with a snake. Everything interested her; nothing, it appears, distressed. She expressed no opinions. Perhaps she didn't have any. I hoped not. Now what a lovely, empty, translucent vessel that would be—a woman without any opinions.

I waited till they left the dining room; then I walked to the gate, hailed a motor scooter and set off to visit Shankar Dhas.

Chapter Two

I HAD LEFT DELHI THE PREVIOUS JUNE IN WHAT MIGHT BE
called emergency conditions—it had been a case of getting
Pamela on the first available plane. I traveled light, so there
wasn't much luggage to store and I left my car with Shankar,
with the stipulation that it was on no account to be driven by
his younger brother, Krishan.

So the fault in the first place was mine. I knew Shankar well,
and I knew the story of his life before I met him. I made the
usual human mistake of disregarding features in his nature
which were not prominent in my own.

Once upon a time Shankar had been one of India's bright
young men with a job on the National Film Board and a promising future opening out before him. Two of his documentary
films had won awards at film festivals and he was beginning to
make a name for himself abroad. I saw those films: they were

made with poor equipment and very little money; they were fresh, rough and honest; and because of them he had the misfortune to win a scholarship jointly sponsored by UNESCO and the Government of India, to study documentary film making in Europe and Canada. He was away for eighteen months, and when he returned to Delhi it was to find that his old job had not been kept open for him as the conditions of his scholarship demanded, but was now occupied by a Calcutta failed B.A., a young man of no ability, who nevertheless enjoyed an attenuated family relationship with the Director.

Well, it was an old story. Six hundred failed B.A.'s and half a dozen jobs. . . . In India the biggest mistake you can make is not to be there.

At length Shankar was shuffled off into an insignificant job with the Publications Division, designing covers for agricultural pamphlets. He had little aptitude for what he was doing and was not liked by his fellow employees, who regarded him as an impostor with some pull higher up. A clerk and a peon who had wanted the job both wrote letters to the Employments Board, complaining that it had not been offered within the Department, and hinting at bribery and nepotism.

But though the muddle of India—the envy, the apathy, the distress of misdirection—might seem to be expressed in Shankar's career, so also was India's peculiar power.

"At first I felt bitterness," he told me. "But now I have overcome all that. I was young and ambitious. . . . I see now that I wanted to be famous. This will teach me a lesson. What was my camera? Only an eye with which to look at life. Have I no other eyes? No other means of expressing myself? I see now that nothing has been taken from me."

I said to him once, "If I bought you a camera, Shankar, and lent you enough money to buy film. . . ." But he wasn't interested any more. He had laid down his ambitions and his talents like offerings at the feet of God, and we both knew that if I lent him money, somebody would very quickly seize it from him.

On his meager salary he supported his wife, Rani, his daughter Mira, his wife's grandmother, who three years before had come on a visit still awaiting its termination, his younger brother, Krishan, who was taking his B.A. at Delhi University, and Rampal, a boy ten years old, the eighth son of an old family servant who had looked after Shankar when he himself was a child. Two other brothers, though theoretically self-supporting, repeatedly called upon his resources from Calcutta. He was constantly lending money to friends and most of it he never saw again. He was hopelessly in debt, but his debts never worried him. He simply borrowed more to pay off the interest on money already borrowed. Sometimes he asked himself what would happen to his family if he should die, and the thought of their impending destitution would make him utterly miserable. But for the most part he was optimistic and happy. He wanted his life snarled up and thick with dilemmas, just as I wanted mine airy and open. I liked to be able to move swiftly and far, without knocking into other human beings, but Shankar needed a dependent on every finger and other people's problems around his neck. I have heard it said that Indians are so unaccustomed to solitude that if they ever find themselves alone, they sing and talk to themselves to reproduce the conditions of normal life and to fill up the terrifying silence. I think it would have frightened Shankar had he found himself leading his life solely for his own gratification.

I first met him at a cocktail party given by the National Film Board to which he had been invited by mistake, the news of his transfer not yet having permeated the department responsible for issuing the invitations. I noticed him immediately. He was rather quiet for an Indian, and this alone made him stand out in that noisy, gesticulating, head-wagging crowd. He stood back against a wall, and he wasn't talking to anyone, just gazing about him. A slight, quiet man. His face looked both vulnerable and strong, and though his large eyes were brimmed with the usual Indian melancholy—that look of unassuageable racial distress —there was also an air of contentment about him. He seemed at peace with himself.

After that night I saw a lot of him. I took to dropping in on him whenever I had an evening to spare, and we would sit talking and arguing as I used to do in my student days.

In every way he was very different from myself, and his qualities—his odd, acute intelligence, his integrity and his gentleness had an exotic flavor and an element of mystery, so that he was always unpredictable and always interesting. But he irritated me too. He made me want to lay hands on his life, to shake him out of habits of kindness and goodness so obsessively pursued they seemed like vices. His willingness in lending himself to be exploited—and why were those friends and kindred who sucked his blood so inferior to Shankar himself?—I would like to have pointed out to him that perhaps he had debased them. . . . And his docile acceptance of misfortune, an Indian quality that the Westerner always abhors, for our whole concept of progress is based on struggle and complaint.

Sometimes I asked myself if he was capable of standing up

and retorting to destiny, and what kind of reverse would sting him into revolt. Something perhaps quite unexpected—possibly, in my estimation, very trivial. For Shankar suffered from a defect in his mental sight, something that was like color blindness in the world of dimension. He could not judge volume, or distance; a bubble would weigh in his hand like a ball of lead; and a mountain, ten miles off, looked to him as insignificant as a grain of sand.

Shankar occupied an apartment in one of the new colonies on Delhi's Agra side. These had sprung up in the matter of a few years and so quickly extended the city's limits they had taken the countryside by surprise. Tombs, wells, whole villages had been swallowed up in the relentless push of houses, roads, bazaars. Cattle, robbed of their pasture, wandered about at night plundering gardens; pigs snuffled in the rubbish dumps and jackals still prowled in what had so recently been their exclusive dominion. There seemed no time for making suitable adjustments, or any room either, for that matter.

Shankar's colony was one of the more recently completed and its newness was daily manifest in the frailty of its public services. The electricity flickered on and off, water taps gaped dry, and the bus service was so inadequate that frequent riots at bus stops had been known to result in fatal injuries. But nothing in India looks new for long, and within a year the buildings had tarnished and slid toward decrepitude. Hardly a blade of green remained to tell that grass had grown there. Trees had been planted but these had either died from lack of water or been eaten by cows, and only rusted tin shields stood to commemorate a vain desire for beauty in some official mind. Two such tin shields deocrated the compound outside Shankar's apartment, and these, along with a red quilted eiderdown that usually hung over his balcony, were the landmarks I looked for in a row of grimy, barrack-like buildings that all looked exactly the same.

He came to the door and seized my hand. He was really delighted to see me. He was looking thinner and older, and I wondered what life had been doing to him while I was away. I supposed that Krishan was the trouble. He usually was.

"But this is marvelous, Richard! It is wonderful to see you again. When did you get back? How is Pamela? Is she with you?"

"She stayed in London."

"Come in! Come in! When you write you must send her my best regards."

Pamela and Shankar got on well together. He liked her and she liked him at a time when India and most Indians repelled her. With Shankar she was relaxed and natural as few people saw her.

We sat on divans—there was also a table in the room and one chair, but nobody ever used it. Three tin trunks filled with books were stacked in one corner. Shankar, Rani and Mira slept in here and Rani's grandmother, Krishan and Rampal occupied a second room.

The flat was filled with a sweet, sickly smell. Rani was cooking something in the kitchen. Shankar called out to her to join us and she made a quick dash into the room, carrying two plates of sweetmeats and holding her head averted. It was Shankar's proud contention that she was emancipated, but her daughter Mira would perform the movements of a freedom which for Rani was largely theoretical.

"By the way," I said, taking a piece of sticky halva, "about the car—"

"It isn't here," said Shankar quickly. "It's in garage being overhauled."

"When will it be ready?"

"Tomorrow, the next day—who can say with these fellows?" His narrow face looked suddenly tense and sad, "If you had only written to me and told me that you were coming, then this inconvenience would not have happened."

I had written to him and he had obviously got my letter because he had answered it; but in India facts have no power in the face of wishes, and nothing is true or false all of the time. Shankar wound one leg around the other and told me that he had been reading one of the new French novelists. "This is heartless stuff, Richard. It is too cerebral. You cannot write a good book without using your heart."

So much for the car. I began to feel alarmed. "You know, it's rather important. I can manage here all right for a day or two, but I have to go to Agra—there's a seminar in one of the colleges and they want me as a visiting lecturer." Next month, but I didn't tell him that.

"You will never get to Agra by car. Roads are broken. Between here and Palwal there are thirty miles of water."

"Not again!" It happened after every monsoon.

"What do you expect?" And he began to speak with biting sarcasm of Government deficiencies. "Do you think Government is going to mend Agra road? Government officials go by plane. Why should they bother about people on the ground? And those fellows mending the roads—they make a lot of money hauling out distressed motorists. It is in their interest keeping the potholes open."

A portrait of Sir Rabindranath Tagore, hanging cockeyed on the wall, looked down on us with foggy sentimental eyes. It had made its appearance in the house the year before at a function to commemorate the poet's birthday, and was still draped with the withered marigold garland that had honored it on that occasion. Shankar, whose nature felt no need for symmetry, had never noticed that the picture hung crooked on the wall and that the garland hung crooked on the picture, but I experienced a subtle discomfort whenever I looked at it.

I looked at it now, and wondered if by getting up and putting it straight I should set my own mind at rest but donate my unease to Shankar. India allows few horizontals, and Indian parallels are forever meeting. . . . For two years now, sensitive to any accusation of racial arrogance, I had been searching for a new world of proportion. But in fact was there one? I sometimes doubted.

And now I found myself thinking of Helen Siegel, crossing the Mayfair lawn—from point A to point B—as straight as an arrow. With one thought in her mind—one simple, luminous thought that had nothing to do with the meaning of truth and the obligations of love.

Pamela used to say that I didn't really like India, that I simply felt that I ought to. Perhaps she was right. But if I didn't like India, at least I liked being there, and her accusation of dishonesty irritated me. She went farther, on occasions when she wanted to hurt me, and said that my friendship with Shankar was a mere sentimental gesture and false in its initial impulses; that Englishmen in India were doing penance for the exclusiveness of their fathers, and that this was only a further condescension.

Running feet sounded on the stairs, and then laughter. A charming, infectious sound, and disturbing too, because you sensed the lightness of control upon it. The next moment Krishan burst in through the door. He paused, looking smilingly about him, to assess what kind of entrance he had made, then flung himself upon me, throwing both arms around my neck.

"Oh, Mr. Mardellis, Mr. Mardellis! How happy I am to see you!"

Shankar laughed too and tugged at his brother's hand. "Krishan! What are you doing? You are pulling Richard to pieces. Come over here. Sit down. Be calm."

"Halva! Rani has been making halva and, brother, you are eating it all when you know it is my favorite."

Shankar watched him with tender, devoted eyes. "Do you think I don't remember? And do you think that Rani would not remember? She is in kitchen and if you ask her you will find she has put a dish aside."

But in came Rani, carrying an enamel dish that was piled with orange halva and topped with a crust of thin silver leaf that fluttered in the moving air.

Krishan flung himself on the divan and sat cross-legged while everything drew toward him and turned about him. Rani, forgetting that my presence embarrassed her, leaned down with the halva dish in her brown, bangled hand; Shankar bent tender, adoring eyes. The old grandmother tottered to the kitchen door and stood grinning with the simple delight of just looking upon that darling, beautiful boy. Even I gave him my stern regard.

Krishan was only seventeen and excessively pretty, but without the dew of freshness that surely should not have dried on so

young a face. His mouth, with its short upper lip deeply in-
dented and tight corners tucked into glossy, round cheeks,
seemed always to smile in a knowing, self-satisfied way; and his
long eyes had the heavy, low lids of an older man, a sensualist
and a profligate. With his springy flesh and bluish, mossy skin,
he looked succulent and edible. Instinctively one dressed him in
cloth of gold and set him down in an Oriental court in the last
orgiastic days before its fall.

"The University is out on strike," said Shankar, his eyes
shining with an admiration that extended toward everything that
Krishan did, even his misdemeanors. "They do not like their
examination papers. What do you think of this, Richard? These
boys do nothing all the year and study the cram books for two
weeks before the exams, and then when the examiner asks them
a question that is not in the cram books they say they have been
cheated. This kind of easy degree—what meaning does it have?
When I took B.A. I had to work hard for it."

Krishan's damp, sugary lips pouted sulkily. "I hope that every
day I will not have to listen to reproaches. I can see that I should
have stayed and supported my friends. Today they are marching
and holding meetings. 'Why do you desert us?' they asked. 'We
must all stick together and stand up for our rights.' 'Because I
must go to elder brother,' I told them. It is always like this. My
heart rules me and my judgment is at fault."

"You must do better than those lazy fellows. All you want is to
enjoy your life, but you do not know the difficulties and the
competition. I shall not always be here to protect you. You must
not waste your opportunities."

"Listen to him. And have you not wasted yours? If you still

had your job with the film unit I could have a room to myself
and air conditioning."

"My life is not important. It is half lived, and yours is only
beginning."

Krishan sighed, his eyes venomous with boredom, and reached
for another piece of halva. But even resentment calls for some
expense of spirit, and as he placed the sweet on his red, wet
tongue, I watched his expression grow contented and satisfied. I
asked myself what he wanted from life and what he would be
doing in ten, in twenty years' time. Though I disliked him, he
interested me. He seemed entirely inert and negative. He would
never act to help himself, but there was a curious power about
him of attracting other people's actions.

Then suddenly he looked up, and I had a very curious experi-
ence—vivid and immediate, like a hallucination. I saw myself
get up, cross the room and, bending down, put my lips on his
mouth.

Krishan smiled, holding his eyelids steady over his old, knowing eyes. "Mr. Mardellis," he said softly, "I hope that you have
not come to take away our car."

"Krishan," cried Shankar, "you will not speak like that! What
are you saying? Is this gratitude?"

"Of course we are grateful, but he is your friend, and does not
friendship mean that we share our possessions? What can he
need with a car? Whereas we are such a long way out. The
buses are no good. I have to wait for two hours sometimes and
then I can't get on. And they are full up with riffraff. I do not
like to stand crushed against common people."

I said nothing, and thought that Krishan, like Shankar, misjudged his distances. His weakness lay in too much daring and too much faith.

Abruptly I got to my feet. Shankar followed me out onto the veranda. "Don't go, Richard. This conversation pains me."

"You're too sensitive."

He did not catch the sarcasm but sorrowfully replied, "He abuses your generosity."

"I told you not to let him use the car," I said curtly. "He's not responsible."

"He must learn responsibility," said Shankar softly. "How can he learn if I do not trust him?"

I turned away and leaned on the balcony railing. The compound below had the melancholy soiled look that falls on all busy places after the crowds have gone. Not a soul moved on the ugly domesticated ground, and the objects decorating it—the two tin shields and a capsized dustbin—stood out with a trenchant vitality, as though they were symbols of some meaning that the scene contained. A piece of white paper fluttered on a thornbush. It wouldn't last the night; some half-starved, wandering cow would soon be after it. Shankar stood silent beside me, and now I felt sorry, knowing I had hurt him.

"He's young," I said.

"He's young!" He snatched for comfort from this platitude, and repeated, "He's very young!"

We arranged to meet the next day at a coffeehouse in town. "The car will be ready," he promised and, striving at the last moment toward some consistency, "I will tell those chaps to get a wiggle on."

But for a moment he had seen Krishan with my eyes and, glancing back to the room, I saw him go in, bend down over that soft, slothful figure and strike him on the cheek. Then he put his arms about him and kissed him. Krishan did not move or speak. Too lethargic and too gluttonous of adulation for any frank expression of his feelings, he remained always, as Shankar said, "a sweet-tempered boy."

It was nearly midnight when I got home; the hotel stood quiet and dark in its circle of trees. Under the light the chaukidar slept, his gaunt face upturned and his eyeballs twitching under their closed lids, as though he were alert for danger in the half light of an anxious dream.

My room was stuffy and hot and smelt faintly of mold, like a warm swamp. I switched on the fan and, as its big black wings slowly turned, a sheet of paper stirred on the carpet by the door.

Welcome home, old dear. I have an exciting new flat ideally situated on an open latrine. I'll be housewarming soon so find me a tabla player. I think I'll go native with Bharata Natya on the roof. Any ideas about that? There's a delicious little thing doing her stuff at the Ashoka, but I don't think I can afford her. Is Pamela with you? Give her my love if she is, and if she isn't come round.

Yours ever,
Giles

I undressed and went into the bathroom. A small room, but exceedingly high, like a corridor standing on end. A sparrow had been nesting on the top of a switch box high up on the wall, and bits of straw lay scattered on the floor. A house lizard darted behind the shaving mirror. Giles' note, bringing Giles to mind, had also brought Pamela, for they belonged to the same period of my life, and to an India which she had managed to infect with her antipathies.

Midnight: the creaking fan moved the air but did not cool it. I lay on my hard, warm bed, extravagantly disposed on the large double sheet. My suitcase was still packed; the big brown furniture standing about the room remained vacant and anonymous. And my solitude rolled back upon me, like a wave of hope.

Chapter Three

MY APPOINTMENT WITH SHANKAR WASN'T TILL TWELVE, BUT
I had to announce myself to Sir Malcolm, so I set off at ten-
thirty and hailed a motor scooter at the hotel gate.

A Sikh picked me up and, seated behind his broad, sweating
back, I watched the trees slide by, and the big, white, pillared
houses. Roads converged into roundabouts that, from a vivid
circle of flowering shrubs, again split up into roads. Signposts
proclaimed a past which in each of its episodes exalts one
segment of Indian life at the expense of another. Akbar,
Tughlak, Wellesley, Aurangzeb—simultanously heroes and op-
pressors, but never one image for all at the same time. At India
Gate, George V, under a red sandstone canopy, stood deprived of
his nose by some student indulging a sense of injustice.

Down King's Way a double row of flags, set out for the visit of
a foreign celebrity, panted in the heavy air, and to the west the
red columns and domes of Lutyens' Secretariat stood diminished

under white turrets of monsoon cloud. More red buildings of later date glowed hot amongst trees in the roads beyond, and in one of these, which also housed a bank and a minor department of a minor Ministry, Sir Malcolm presided over the U.N. Office.

Sir Malcolm was not unapproachable, but he worked defended, as it were, by his Indian secretary, Ruplal, and his American assistant, Hilton Chase.

Ruplal's position as seen from within the office was relatively humble, his power evident only to an outsider like myself, who, if I wanted anything, had either to conciliate or circumvent him. It paid to be his friend, and I was not, having fallen out with him during the first year of my assignment when he had tried to maneuver me into one of the current rackets.

Hilton, ex-Harvard, ex-New York Office, was young, delicately bred, richly raised. A boy with a conscience, doing his first field job with touching enthusiasm. I liked him, though liking Americans wasn't fashionable at that time. His wide gray eyes looked about him with such candor and surprise that his being in India at all seemed like an act of valor, commanding respect.

That morning Ruplal was out and Hilton in, so I was shown through to the great man.

He sat at a large desk, a picture of Nehru and a map of India hanging on the wall behind that long, thin-cheeked, horsy head.

We shook hands and said what we had to say. "I'm sorry I had to take that extra leave."

"Quite all right. Quite all right."

He was stiff and embarrassed. He had little social ease on any occasion and my troubles had discomforted him. I felt that in his view I had committed a breach of good form, and that he disliked me now.

The feeling was mutual. Professionally I respected him, but I had had to put my cards on the table, and now I couldn't forgive him for having seen more of my life than I normally showed. I found it hard to look in his eyes, so I stared into them more straightly than was necessary; and he stared back into mine, so that we were locked together in a kind of fruitless and unwilling enmity.

"I take it you're on your own?" And then, as though to reassure me that the question was official and that he wasn't prying into my affairs, he murmured vaguely. "The allowance . . ."

Yes, I was alone.

"How are things at the College?"

I said I'd spoken to Prasad on the telephone but hadn't been there yet. I'd only been back for a day and what with transport . . .

He perked up and looked concerned. By the terms of our contract, transport for the Experts was the responsibility of the Indian Government, and there had been a six months' quarrel with the Ministry about it when I first arrived. Sir Malcolm had halfheartedly and unsuccessfully tried to settle it, and I had ended up by importing my own car. "Where's your car?"

"It's being serviced. I'm supposed to be picking it up this morning. But you know . . ."

He knew.

"If you've got some transport here you could let me have for a day or two. . . ."

He didn't think he had, but he'd do his best. If I was stuck perhaps I'd let him know.

In the compound outside, Rajasthani women in swinging red petticoats bent with their bundles of twigs to scrape patterns in the dust. My Sikh driver was waiting, though I had already paid him off.

"I'm going to walk." Which I did, under trees that shook with crows and cast a watery shadow on the path. Out in the chaotic road, bicycles, bullock carts and a cow or two dozed and wandered. My Sikh kept to my side and, ignoring the signals of needy pedestrians, pestered me down the length of the road.

In Connaught Circus rattan blinds flapped against the white pillars and cast black, brutal shadows on the walls. From a stall displaying ivory and sandalwood boxes incense coiled in the air like a spectral snake. A small boy with one eye stretched out his arms festooned with jasmine flowers. He followed me for half a block, scenting the hot, wet air in the grimy aisles, and I remembered how I had bought a jasmine garland for Pamela, perhaps from this same importunate child, in those far-off days when, fresh and excited, she had seemed prepared to take a hesitant step toward this most difficult and yet most lovable country.

The colonnades of the Circus turned graciously westward, architecturally pleasing, but smudged and soiled by the touch of India. Anonymous brown stains that grow out of the base of all Indian buildings had seeped up the columns like an excretion from the earth. Big, gay signs hung at wild angles. I remembered how we had laughed at the hopeful, grandiloquent names—the K. Walitys, the Ivory Markets, and the Art Palaces. I had still been working at my marriage then; now I had shuffled it onto the perimeter of my life and all I wanted, or thought I wanted, was to be able to hold the center alone.

I arrived at the Supreme Coffee House a little early. The proprietor, seeing me come in and responding to an instinct still alive from the past, dispersed some noisy youths and gave me their table.

Fans turned, stirring the thick, dark air. The scene wagged with black beards and fluttered with long, illustrative hands. Turbans, pink, yellow, white and green, dotted the gloom like flowers. There was not a woman in sight. Only men—all of them talking, none of them listening, and none of them Shankar.

I waited half an hour and still he did not come. Why? Heaven alone knew. Some mystery. No car—not today at any rate, perhaps not tomorrow. Perhaps never again. And I was angry.

I took a motor rickshaw and rattled home behind the sweating shoulders and apricot turban of yet another Sikh. When I got back to the hotel it was past noon and oppressively hot. Above, the sky had whitened, seemed now not a sky at all but a glaring gap—a hole torn in the firmament. Nothing—not even the trees—looked beautiful and everything looked bored. The lawn was a stagnant pool and the birds, stunned by the heat, were silent. It had been a typical Indian morning. No achievement in any direction, and nothing to show but a loss of energy and a souring temper.

I was late in to lunch and the table where the Siegels had been sitting the night before had been cleared away. I was still angry and, in my resentful, in-turned mood, disposed to chew over my grievances.

I knew I had been a fool for letting Shankar have the car and at the same time trying to protect it by imposing prohibitions he could not respect. Shankar could not act in isolation; he was not an individual, he was a society, and everything he possessed belonged to everyone he loved. Mine had been one of those essentially selfish gestures—feeling the pressure of affection within me, I had evacuated an unwanted gift and landed my victim with responsibilities he was not prepared to accept. The sort of sloppy feeling and messy, dishonest behavior I detested in other people; the sort of action that was always getting Pamela into trouble. In fact, it was a bit Indian.

"My God! It's you! Why on earth have you come back to this bloody country?" Soni's son Ram Chandra came across the room and pulled up a chair. He was all fresh from the dhobi and the coconut-oil bottle, his hair arranged in stiff ebony waves and a yellow paisley scarf knotted at his throat.

I quite liked Ram Chandra, though he was as unreliable and neurotic as only an Indian can be. His elder brother had been abroad, but had showed such unnatural independence on his return that Soni had decided it wiser to keep Ram Chandra on the chain.

"Why don't you clear out?" I asked him once.

"Are you mad? Just look at me. I do exactly as Daddy says. I'm afraid to say boo to a goose. It's all very well for you chaps chucked out on the football field before you can walk, but I'm quite effete—quite, quite effete."

This was his chosen role and he played it, in all its New Delhi variations. He dabbled in the arts, was a member of the Delhi theatre group, and organized little shows of music and Bharata Natya. He could hardly be said to have any friends, but he knew a large number of people in the European and American communities and was forever picking one up, dropping him or her, picking up another, quarreling, separating, reuniting. At that time he had quarreled with almost everyone he knew and was consequently delighted to see me. Straightaway he set about telling me that I was the only foreigner in the whole of New Delhi worth knowing. The rest were impossible. They either ganged up together and lived off canned food or sat at the feet of Vinoba Bhave and talked a lot of twaddle about Ahimsa and the Upanishads. Except Giles, of course, but India's sanitary arrangements had got him down. He was obsessed with lavatories.

I said, "He's taken a flat. Have you seen it?"

"Not yet. How's Pamela? Is she with you?"

"No, she stayed in London. She may come out when it gets cooler."

"She'll be all right here. Daddy's put air conditioning in the new annex and he won't allow cats. He says they eat the birds."

At first I felt surprise—that violent, kick-in-the-belly astonishment that leaves you feeling void and sick. Then anger, directed less at the kick itself than at the unfairness of being unprepared for it, of having lived for so long in ridiculous ignorance.

My face must have given me away, for his confidence faltered and he became too casual for words. "Oh, you don't have to worry. I heard the whole thing. Giles told me."

"Told you what?"

"What?"

"Giles."

"About that place in Benares and how you had to get rid of a hundred cats."

"Twenty-eight."

"I thought it was thirty-eight. . . . *Do* say it was thirty-eight! *Don't* disillusion me! It's such a perfectly marvelous story."

I got up then and walked away, in case I should say something cruel and unjust.

He called out after me. "Well, you damned well needn't take it out on me. He's told everyone in Delhi. It's the big joke."

I walked down the veranda, the lawn on my right steaming in the heat, and the sky white and ugly. The mallee crouched by a bed of canna lilies, as though brought to his knees by the weight of the air. A screen door opened and the old dhobi came out, carrying a bundle of sheets over his back.

"Tika, sahib?"

"Tika."

He looked too old to be alive. No teeth. Knotty, sparrow-like bones held together in a wrinkled brown bag of skin. His eyes yellowed and dim. But his grin was saucy and undefeatable; his "tika, sahib" air open impertinence. You felt that life had hammered him into such a steely substance even the worst misfortunes would barely dent him. And I went on into my room, thinking of Pamela, who was composed of such receptive stuff that a breath of derision would reach her over half the world.

I don't care what sort of a fool I look or what kind of failure people think me. I have made my own assessment of my qualities and there's not a great deal in it that needs defending. The most esteemed virtues don't appeal to me much; I'm happy to settle for honesty, and leave it at that. But Pamela took from me all I disclaimed for myself. Someone, it seemed, had to defend her. Perhaps, loyalty being all I could give, I gave it to excess, or perhaps I was keeping her as my own exclusive victim. It hardly matters; dissect any impulse and you will find yourself with some unattractive ingredients. I felt guilty then, angry and revengeful. And I felt an aching compassion which is my substitute for love.

I went to my desk. I wanted to call Prasad but I could never remember the number, and when I found my address book and went out again a car had drawn up on the drive. It was one of Sir Malcolm's office cars, and Fred Siegel, wearing a new white tropical suit, briefcase in hand, was getting into it. That didn't please me too much either.

Chapter Four

THE TELEPHONE WAS IN THE MANAGER'S OFFICE, AND THE Manager, Agawalla, was a relative of Soni's—a small, indigent-looking man with the apologetic, ingratiating manner of one who is always making promises that cannot be fulfilled. His clothes were shabby and dirty and he shaved about once a fortnight, using castoff razor blades that the bearers collected from the guests' rooms. Day and night his eyes had a strained, shrinking look, as though life glared in his face like the noonday sun.

Soni had supplied him with a small cubicle next to the dining room, and equipped it with a desk and chair. Here he was to be found most of the day, soaking up, like a sponge, the complaints of residents. He shouted orders at the servants, which no one obeyed, for they carried little authority with them. He listened, he replied. He said, "Yes, yes. Acha! Acha! I will do that."

Agawalla's office was so confined that if anyone wanted to go in there to use the telephone, Agawalla had to get up and go out. This exodus, however, seemed only partial, and you had an impression of fighting for space in the dense, hot air. That day, as usual, the floor had not been swept, and Agawalla's sandals lay dispersed upon it. The desk was littered with grimy papers, some undelivered letters, the ancient rocky sections of a cut-up lime, and a dirty teacup, which, when I tried to push it out of the way, proved to be welded by time to the top of the desk.

Prasad didn't seem perturbed over my transport problem, or disposed to help. He told me gently that I needed a day or two to settle down. I must be tired after my journey, and in any case it was nearly the end of the week (it was Tuesday) and, valuable as my work was, and anxious as they all were to see me, etc., etc. As most Experts in India are only wanted for the scholarships and equipment that go with them, he had been enjoying my four months' absence and was keen to extend it as long as he could.

I rang Sir Malcolm, but got no further than Ruplal, who told me Sir Malcolm was still at lunch. "We are very pleased to know you are safely returned, sir," he said in his most unctuous voice.

I hung up and rang the office again. This time I asked to speak to Hilton Chase. We chatted a bit. I told him what I wanted and it turned out that Sir Malcolm had been in his office for the past half hour.

I said, "You know, our friend stops a lot of calls when he doesn't like the voice on the other end."

Hilton was astonished. "Richard, you must be wrong. Ruplal is *invaluable*. He's one of our most trusted people. He just *runs* the place. There must be some explanation."

All foreigners in India begin to look alike after a while; they are worn down to the same forms by the frictions of Indian life, like stones tumbled and polished on the bed of a river. Our differences erased, we are left with the one thing we all have in common, our new salient feature, the fact of our not being Indian. I had been watching for this process to show itself in Hilton, but so far he was holding out against it. No word of complaint or cynical pronouncement ever passed his lips. My cynicism on the other hand saddened him, and he was forever crusading against it.

"You underestimate him, Richard," he earnestly said. "You really do."

At length I was talking to Sir Malcolm, but the whole circuitous operation was a waste of time. All the cars were out for the afternoon, he said, but he would instruct Ruplal to send me one in the morning.

I decided to ring Shankar, but I had tried this difficult operation several times in the past and had a fair idea how it would turn out. Was that Publications? Yes, this was Publications. Who did I want? I wanted the Agricultural Section. Was this Agriculture? No, it was Publications. But was it the Agricultural Section of Publications? No. It was Medicine. At length, filtering back and forth through the switch, I got on to Agriculture. Could I speak to Shankar Dhas? The voice on the end of the phone had never heard of him and said, "Ring again tomorrow."

"What is the good of my ringing tomorrow if you've never heard of him?"

"Ring tomorrow. That man will be back."

I said, "He occupies a desk in Dr. Batterjee's office."

So I wanted to speak to Dr. Batterjee, did I, asked the voice in a tone of relief. No, I didn't, but nevertheless found myself doing so.

"Sir," said Dr. Batterjee, "it is unwise to put your faith in mechanical inventions. We in India do not trust machinery. We trust in God and the life of the spirit. All else is worthless. Why do you not visit your friend and talk to him face to face? This is the only way to settle anything."

At length somebody said in a loud voice. "He has gone away."

I said, "I want to speak to Shankar Dhas. Hullo! Who is that?"

It was a voice, very far away, and it sounded like Shankar. We were cut off.

I hung up, reflecting that although in India you never got what you wanted, you never went away empty-handed. I had enjoyed my conversation with Dr. Batterjee.

Agawalla followed me down the veranda. "Mr. Mardellis, Mr. Mardellis. You are wanted on the telephone."

I went back to the grimy papers, the undisplaceable teacup and the squeezed lime.

It was Giles. It gave me quite a jolt, hearing that high, thin voice.

"Why aren't I seeing you? Did you get my note?"

"Yes."

"What's the matter? You sound frightfully far away."

"It's the phone."

"Come over and have a drink this evening. I might even rustle you up a curry. I can't guarantee what it will be like, I'm just working through my *third* cook, but it couldn't be worse than that muck Soni gives you."

"Look, Giles, I've got a lot to do. I haven't even unpacked yet. I'll see you later."

But he was rambling on like an old woman about his servant problems. He'd got a cook, bearer, sweeper, dhobi, mallee, chaukidar, the *lot*. All filthy and villainously ugly, and he just knew they were plucking him naked. The tea, the sugar, the tins of *dalda*. A little stall that wasn't there last week had suddenly appeared in the lane by the back gate. Tea, roasted gram, those orange sugary sweets you fried in ghee. He suspected his cook was setting up the family in business. "What I really want is a Number One boy."

"That's China. You're in the wrong country."

"Well, I don't see why the system shouldn't be introduced here. Someone a bit higher up in the social scale who'll protect me from this gang so that I don't have to go through the squalid business of sacking them and stripping their uniforms off them before they go. A sort of private-secretary-*cum*-housekeeper. He could do all that and get me new ones and I needn't even know."

"You're mad. That would be one more eating you alive. What do you want a chaukidar for? Get yourself one good cook-bearer, ex-Army, from the hills. Get rid of the rest of them."

"My dear fellow, the moment a European sets foot in India at least a hundred Indians begin to live off him. This is his destiny and his duty. The thing is to keep alive. One does want a little flesh on one's own bones. A failed B.A., that's what I want. I could get rid of my driver and he could look after the car and tootle me around. . . ."

Back in my room I undressed and took a shower. Most of the holes in the sprinkler were blocked, and a steaming-hot dribble fell on the back of my neck. The lizard had moved onto the ceiling and hung above my head, its pink transparent body filled with the dark clot of its dinner.

I sat down on my bed and started a letter to Pamela.

"Dear Pamela. . . ." But I had only to write those two words and I was floundering about, looking for something to say.

During the twelve years of our marriage a substantial correspondence had passed between us. There *were* terms under which we could communicate. Pamela could express her grievances fluently and I could present my defense with irony and passion. But we needed the subject of my inadequacy to get us going. Her first letter would probably raise it, but without this to work on I had nothing to say. Only feelings I could not express.

Guilt. Remorse. And a nagging resentment when something happened to show me how fused we were, how she had hooked her sufferings into my flesh. Yet what did they amount to? No real malady, no treatable neurosis. Sometimes I saw them as nothing more than greedy, public gestures. A tug on my sleeve, a handkerchief waving from the other side of the valley. . . . Look. Here I am! Look at me. Watch me! Never forget me.

"Dear Pamela." How inadequate, for, as she had once pointed out to me, I wrote "Dear Sir" to my bank manager and to the estate agent who looked after our flat. But "dearest Pamela" had laid me open to the charge of hypocrisy.

The letter limped on. How was she? Was she looking after herself? Had the headaches gone? I hoped her painting was going well, she was always happy when she was working. It began to sound like a letter of condolence to someone bereaved and I tore it up.

Dear Pamela,

I've just come back from New Delhi. I spent the morning wandering round Connaught Circus waiting for Shankar, who, needless to say, didn't turn up. He seems to have "mislaid" the car. I rather think he let Krishan have it and the darling boy has probably driven it into a tree. . . .

That was better. . . . Stick to me. It sounded more natural, seeing I was supposed to be so wrapped up in myself. But I couldn't leave her out altogether so ended on a solemn moral note.

I've been thinking a lot today about what happened to you in Benares. I feel that the whole trouble with India is that she takes hold of our beliefs and stretches them to a point where they become so ludicrous that we can no longer maintain them. And this is frightening. It's always frightening, suddenly, to be stripped of your convictions. India's extravagances, her extreme postulations, are always logical; that's what takes us unawares, because we'll always pursue a logical deduction. Other cultures let us off lightly; we're not used to being subjected to such stringent tests. When we say we won't take life, we usually mean that we won't resort to killing our neighbors, or, if we're really fanatical, we become vegetarian, or refuse to practice birth control. But we don't mean that we'll meekly sit back and allow a plague of monkeys to devour our melon crop, that we'll spare the lives of cockroaches and centipedes, and wear gauze masks over our mouths so that minute particles of life floating in the air won't fall victim to our gastric juices.

To survive out here, what you have to do, simply, is to dig your toes in, and refuse to be pushed into these ultimate, untenable positions. It's easy for me. I don't believe in anything very strongly —I can shift my stand. But a person like you, a sensitive idealist with strong feelings, is fair game. Isn't that what happened? It was the logical consequence of your desire to look after one destitute animal. And although it was terrible in a way, it was ridiculous too. . . .

Chapter Five

FRED SIEGEL OPENED THE DOOR. "COME IN. COME IN." HE HAD just had a shower and smelt of hair oil and shaving lotion. "Elly, he is here. Dick has come!"

Suddenly my heart was thudding and my throat felt tight. I had not given her a thought all day, yet the moment was large and slow as though I had been waiting for it, storing the hours up behind it.

She stood across the room on the other side of twin beds with green hand-loomed covers, and she was pouring medicine from a brown bottle into a spoon. The air conditioning hummed from the blocked-up window, filling the room with a low, dull din that made me feel I had gone deaf and, through the dulling of this one sense, laid a fog of unreality on the others. I knew these air-conditioned limbos and their power for inducing irresponsible acts and rash confessions.

A year before, a girl I had known for an evening said to me,

"When I was seven I took a carving knife and tried to kill my father." Her voice came to me thinly over the roar, and suddenly it seemed like the last day on earth, so I made love to her, my mind obsessed by thoughts of mortality. It was the beginning of that particular affair, and next day I felt surprised that what had happened in that room should have any consequence outside it.

"Here you are, Fred. Drink that."

Pamela would have looked up when I came in, spilled the medicine and made me feel a brute for arriving at the wrong moment. But Helen kept her eyes bent to the spoon, and only when she had handed it to Fred did I get my smile. "Sit down. Sit on the bed."

"Give him a chair, Elly. Let Dick have a chair."

"They are designed for Hindu penitents. He doesn't look to me like a penitent."

"I'm not."

"Of course he's not. Sit on the bed. *Lie* on the bed."

I sat, and she stood smiling at me as if she had achieved something. I said, "Do you like it here?"

"Of course." The question seemed to astonish her. Doesn't everyone like it everywhere? She seemed totally unconscious of the areas of darkness looming behind her own bright place in the sun. Her expression was friendly and warm—but unsubtle, unequivocal, uninviting—and I thought to myself that she had never known passion. The thought turned my eyes to Fred, and I wondered what love would be between them, and then felt resentment, as though he were the seducer, preying upon something already mine.

"What will you have?" he asked. "Scotch, or Indian gin."

"Indian gin. Scotch would spoil my palate."

But he wouldn't hear of it. I must have Scotch, and then I had to be told all over again about how he had got it from this friend Otto, in the German Embassy, because, in case I hadn't guessed, he was of German extraction, and had come to New Delhi with letters of introduction.

He talked excitedly, wearing all the time that big, blank smile. With Fred you had to feel you were having a terrific time and, to every occasion in which he took part, he gave far more boost than it could carry. I wondered about the medicine he had been taking and suspected it to be some G.P.'s harmless prescription for an overstrained temperament. His manner had the jumped-up ebullience that is often accompanied by bouts of despair. There was an intermittent, compulsive flicker on the edge of his smile.

Helen sat down on the other side of the bed and began turning the pages of a magazine. She wore a putty-colored raw-silk dress, cut low at the back, and the overhead light dropped two burnished spots on her shoulders. A big, square zircon flashed on her hand—she had the strong, tapering fingers that can support these cumbersome stones, and long, bony wrists. I wanted to talk to her but I didn't know what to say. She seemed to have given us up for a world of colored pictures and stories with happy endings. Looking over her shoulder, I saw a Kathakali dancer with a huge swirling skirt and painted mask.

"Have you seen any Indian dancing?" I asked her.

"Once. In Melbourne. It was *wonderful!*"

Fred prattled on about the Germans. "Zey are a nice crowd. Awfully hospitable. Zey have invited us twice, haven't they, Elly?"

I looked at her shoulders and the falling line of her dress. And

I felt my blood turn sweet. Fred was such a fool and such a bore I didn't even bother not to stare. The Australians, he declared, were also a "nice crowd," but by the dying fall of his enthusiasm, I gathered they had not come good with duty-free Scotch.

"Otto says he will let me have two bottles a month."

I said, "You know these Embassy chaps can get into trouble if they give their liquor away. If I were you I wouldn't tell too many people."

"But I can tell *you*. *You* wouldn't talk about it."

And why, I thought, shouldn't I violate a secret that has been raped once already? In a way this was his charm. There was nothing furtive about him. He was bubbling over with all his little off-color successes.

"Everyone has been so kind to us, haven't they, Elly? You know we haven't got a car yet, and Sir Malcolm has always provided one when we have asked. This afternoon we drove out to the Qutb Minar and had a look around the gardens. Then we went into Old Delhi through the bazaars. . . ."

Helen was in Agra now, gazing at the marble loveliness of Itma-ud-Daula's tomb. "Like a trinket box on the dressing table of a lady of pleasure." The words floated lazily onto my mind and I tried to remember who had written them. The air conditioner hummed. I felt drowsy, contented and sensual. Fred's voice buzzed around us like a summer fly.

"Zis chap Ruplal, Sir Malcolm's secretary, has been most helpful. Hasn't he, Elly? He has given me quite a lot of useful information. You know I ordered a Mercedes in Germany, and it ought to be arriving in Bombay next month. I wanted to ask you about this. . . ."

Now we had got around to the reason for my being there,

sitting on his bed and drinking his hard-won Scotch. I had a car, didn't I? I had been in India for two years and I must know the ropes.

Ruplal had told him that if he sold his car in New Delhi he would get a good profit, and what's more the kind, accommodating fellow had agreed to see to the whole transaction. I wondered if I should warn him about Ruplal but decided to let him learn the hard way.

"You would have to pay the duty."

"Even so, he says I should get five thousand rupees."

"Then you won't have a car."

"I thought if I could get to Singapore . . ."

I said, "You know, the Indian Government frowns on this sort of thing. They think it's an abuse of our privileges."

"Ruplal says it's perfectly legal."

"What do you think of this?" I said to Helen.

She looked up from her magazine with an expression of surprise. "Oh, I don't know. . . ."

She had never thought about it. It never occurred to her to pass judgment on anyone else's behavior, or to accept responsibility for someone else's actions. A peculiarly uncontemporary personality, I thought. Pamela would have called her coarse and unimaginative, but unlike Pamela there was no contempt in her nature, and she did not waste her intelligence in denying the obvious.

Later we went across to the dining room, and after dinner we sat on the lawn, drinking coffee. We pulled our chairs out into the dark, away from the tumult of insects that spun in futile circles around the veranda lights. Frogs sang in the green damp of the lawn. We could hear the clop of hoofs as bullocks went by, drawing their creeking wooden carts, and far off the swirling, nasal rhythm of marriage music.

She sat beside me—silent for the most part—so there wasn't much call for me to turn and look at her. But I could see her thin brown arms, shining like silk. Fine, pure silk, against the rough, raw silk of her dress.

I wondered if she knew that I was thinking of her. Probably not, for to know would have been to think of me. And she was not thinking of me. Not now. Not yet. It has been said that you can only fall in love with someone who is looking for love themselves. But Helen wasn't looking for anything. She had long ago fortified herself to stand alone, like a tower on a plain. You could walk right around her. I have walked around several women, and at some point have always encountered obscurities —an area of shadow that is cast upon them by another relationship—a place where they are not wholly themselves. But every facet of Helen seemed distinct; every part of her her own possession.

Chapter Six

Next morning at ten-thirty i rang sir malcolm's office and asked to speak to Hilton.

I was angry and he got the edge of my irritation. "I've been waiting for two hours, the car isn't here, and I want to know why I couldn't get to work yesterday afternoon when your transport was joy riding around the Qutb and the Delhi bazaars."

But I'd spoken too strongly and he answered me stiffly. "You know, Richard, I don't deal with transport, but I know those boys have their problems. It's not easy. The drivers are always disappearing for a cup of char. I'll put you through to Ruplal. You can talk to him."

I hung up, but my outburst had its effect, and half an hour later a car arrived.

The College to which I had been assigned did not exist physically at all. A plan had formed in the Ministerial brain, but this inert organ seemed reluctant to project it forth. Besides, there was no money. So our project continued in so-called temporary accommodation—a zamindar's house in a village about twelve miles from Delhi, just off the Gurgaon road, where a staff of five Indians, Prasad and myself instructed thirty students in the arts of Community Development.

To get to the College you had to drive out past Mehrauli and the Qutb Minar, that tall, fluted tower, pink as a stick of rhubarb, that features on every Indian travel brochure. Here previous Delhis lie interred—fort upon fort, mosque upon mosque and, back before Islam and the plundering Afghan kings, temple upon temple. It is one of the spots to go and see. Indian families picnic in the Qutb gardens, the women dressed in their brightest holiday clothes and the children beribboned and satin-clad. On Sunday afternoons they cram the motor scooters like bunches of gaudy, sad-faced flowers, or toss about in garis, drawn by tired, bony horses.

Five departed Delhis, one guidebook will tell you. Another says there are six, and one lays claim to eight. Indian history is too abundant to be accurate.

"You Europeans," Ram Chandra said to me once, when I accused him of being sloppy with facts, "are always ticking off your silly little centuries. You're just like children. . . . So few things have happened to you you remember them all. You write them all down in your little diaries. We don't have to bother with all that."

Beyond Mehrauli the land flattens and settles down into the monotony of the northern plain. Here history disappears, and only geography remains. Rock, dust, mud and weather. . . . It always seemed appropriate to me that I should salute the ghosts of India's conquerors before turning off the road to grapple myself with everything that defeated them.

Our village wasn't poor, as Indian villages go; in fact, being near to Delhi, it was fairly prosperous. But after working in it for six months or so, something, I can only say, died within me. I won't be so banal as to call it innocence. I think of it more as a kind of virtue—if virtue has affinities with hope, and we are told that it has.

Something, somewhere has gone wrong if we can't get to the end of life with our eyes wide open, and nothing is more pathetic than an aging Peter Pan, still piping the slogans of his youth—for hasn't he turned his back on knowledge and resisted growth? But knowledge that falls too swiftly can strike its victim like a curse in a fairy tale. Might it not have been the stroke of some catastrophic enlightenment that put the princess to sleep, or locked her away at the top of the glass hill? Knowledge can overpower and paralyze. And India abounds in paralyzed men.

I sometimes talked to Shankar about my work. Somewhat cynically on the whole. I did not realize how he took my words in and to what unexpected uses he would put them.

"It's all nonsense, Shankar. A waste of our money and your time. . . . You can't help people. There always comes a time when they have to do without you and then it's their level they'll find, not yours. I tell your village people they ought to build drains because I happen to know that open drains will contaminate their water and because I personally don't like living in a stench. But *they* don't mind. They're polite, and they want to please me, so sometimes they do as I say, but how long do you suppose my drains will last? Three, four years after I've gone? I don't know why history doesn't teach us these things. When the Romans came to Britain they had central heating. That's two thousand years ago, and the English are only just getting around to it now."

I left the car in the center of the village near a mosque, where nobody worshiped, for here no Moslems remained. The village street trailed into the sun, a shining dribble of filth—as will have been deduced from my remarks to Shankar, in spite of its three years of improving presence, the College had not managed to achieve drains. However—what with visiting V.I.P.s, sociologists, evaluators, Ministers and tourists from Delhi—begging was very much on the increase. Half a dozen ragged children followed me from the car, dabbing my sleeve with their soft, greasy little paws and whining in flat, dehumanized voices.

They left me at the entrance to a lane, and I went on alone between walls ten feet high, enclosing a space so narrow that no sunlight fell into it. An archway, faced with white plaster, spanned the shadow beneath, and on the lintel two peacocks, one on either side, roughly fashioned in relief had been painted in cobalt blue. Stone steps led to a heavy wooden door that was carved and studded with iron nails and that opened onto a courtyard within. Here the walls rose up on either side, with stairways and balconies. At one corner grew a peepul tree, big and very old, perhaps as old as the house itself. Bending over the court, it threw upon the white sun-struck walls a persistently trembling and quivering web of shade. Sometimes we took lectures out here, and would sit under the peepul tree, with the students in their white clothes squatting on big woven mats. It was a quiet, dignified place, and it had a quality belonging to certain tombs and temples where now only a few village people go, of seclusion and secrecy, in a vast, exposed, unsecret land where human thoughts and actions are continually overflowing and inundating one another.

I arrived at the end of the ten-thirty lectures and spent the morning talking to Dr. Gopal—toothy and hopeless, tremendously likable—and my counterpart, Raja, a young man with a clever, bitter mind, tortured by fears and grumbling with jealousies. Excitedly they told me all their gossip; the visit from the Minister, the letters from last year's scholarship students, the American sociologist who had left them with an astounding questionnaire. . . .

"What are your relations with your students, people-to-people-wise?"

"How many people have smiled at you within the past two hours?"

I didn't see Prasad till lunch, when we all sat at long tables eating the vegetarian foods, the rice, curry and dhal, which were served every day to students and staff. Prasad sat at the end of the table and I took my usual place on his right. He was in a peculiar mood. I had expected that, like the others, he would express some pleasure in having me back. But he hardly spoke to me, carrying on instead a long conversation in Hindi with Dr. Gopal.

Prasad was a Mahratti—one of those hardy, soldierly people who for centuries harassed the Moguls from the south. He had a tall, erect body and a beautiful, severe face—clean-shaven, and crowned by a cap of thick silver hair. It was said that he was quite wealthy, but there was no evidence of money in his appearance or his way of life. He usually wore white trousers and a long gray coat that was frayed at the cuffs and rather dirty. He was an inveterate pan chewer, and a dark sediment filled the cracks in his lips like dried blood. He was highly intelligent, patient and subtle; perhaps I credited him with too much subtlety.

Some weeks later he told me casually that the Ministry was considering an alternative plan for the new College, and was thinking of shifting the project to Madhya Pradesh. He had just heard the news at that time and was disconcerted by it. As UNESCO was putting up half the finance it was very much my affair, and he didn't want me to know about it until he had thought it all out and decided where his interests lay, and what his moves ought to be.

After lunch I went into his office and tried to talk to him. He wasn't discourteous, he just wasn't there. It seemed to me that on the first day of my return he ought to have been, and I was disappointed. I held Prasad in great esteem. I was fond of him too.

I told him about Shankar and my transport problem. "I can't get anything out of him," I said. "I don't want to offend him—on the other hand I simply must get hold of my car. You were saying that the two jeeps . . ."

"True friendship," said Prasad, "is one of life's most treasured possessions. There is nothing like a good friend, unless it is a good book."

"Yes, but if I go on fostering this precious friendship I don't get to work."

"Mr. Mardellis, why are you in such a hurry? A day or two, what does it matter? Indian civilization is five thousand years old. You know it is all the hurrying about in the West that has brought out this great rash of psychiatrists. You should chew pan—it is very soothing to the nerves—and you should adopt a vegetarian diet. The trouble with eating meat is that it makes the blood hot. Rice, dhal and curd provide a very good diet for a man of your temperament. It is blood-cooling and will supply all the nourishment you require. Moreover, excessive meat-eating results in quick deterioration of the eyesight. Look at all those spectacled Americans. Mr. Mardellis, have you ever been to Kashmir?"

"No, I haven't."

"You should go. It is a most beautiful country, and there you will see not one man wearing spectacles nor any blindness even in people of advanced age—and there are men in Kashmir who are a hundred and twenty years old. It is rice, dhal and *curd,* Mr. Mardellis."

"Mr. Prasad, I have an obligation to the institution that employs me. I cannot take money for nothing. That would be corrupt."

"But they are in Paris," he told me gently, "and this is India. Are you not told to adjust yourself to the temperament of the people with whom you are working?"

I considered this, and conceded that yes, I was in India. But at the same time I had my own identity, formed, however, imperfectly in the past and clinging to me like a shadow. "Suppose I stayed in the hotel for the next month, how would I reconcile this neglect of my work with my Christian conscience?"

Prasad closed his eyes for a moment and when he opened them his expression was so remote I felt he had lost consciousness of my presence. He said, "Why don't you get a bicycle?"

The suggestion disconcerted me. I had never thought of it. Why not? After all it was only twelve miles.

"You see," he said, smiling, "our problems are never without solution. But this would not do." And with some really acrobatic Indian logic, he concluded. "It would be an insult to the Indian Government, which has contracted to provide you with a car to your place of work."

On the way home that evening, I told the driver to stop at Shankar's flat. I knocked; there was a sound of scuffling within and I thought I heard his voice. I knocked again.

After a few moments Rani appeared and, standing in the doorway, nodded, smiled and said, "Yes, yes," which is the instinctive Indian response to any situation that has got out of hand.

Unshakable optimism, stubborn mechanical statements of affirmation. Everything is all right, everyone is happy, all will be well. . . . "Yes, yes."

Rani was rather beautiful, with fine, classical features and splendid eyes, but she had the heavy, stupid look of a creature without desires of her own. She looked as if she had been put in the doorway and would stay there until she was taken away.

Was Shankar at home? No reply. When would he be back? Smiling, she shook her head. Would he be back tonight? Would he be here at this time tomorrow? Silence. You don't know? A nod. "Yes, yes."

I asked her if she had a sheet of paper, but the word wasn't in her vocabulary, and when I said it in Hindi, she put her tiny, bangled hand over her mouth and giggled. She came from Madras and probably didn't speak any Hindi anyway. I tore two pages from the back of my diary and scribbled a note.

DEAR SHANKAR,

Sorry I missed you at the coffeehouse. I really am in dire need of the car and would like to know which garage has got hold of it. Naturally any expense incurred must be mine. . . .

I stopped, and a feeling of hopelessness came over me, dulling my mind, like a sudden wave of oppression in the atmosphere. The only solution seemed an Indian one. Give up. Go away. Do something else. But I was not Indian and, as I had said to Prasad that afternoon, my identity dogged me—nagging, worrying, wanting the satisfactions I had been raised to expect. Achievements . . . solutions. . . .

A friend of mine is looking for a private secretary and I suggested that Krishan might do. The work would be light, more of a social nature from what I can gather. He wants someone to manage his household, his private correspondence and drive his car. I feel it would relieve some of the burden you're carrying and, let's face it, Shankar, Krishan will never get a Government job without his B.A.; and he'll never get his B.A. the way he's going.

I thought of underlining the words "and drive his car," but decided this would be going too far, even in a country where everyone overplayed his hand. So, giving Rani my note—my casual message to the Eumenides—I went back to the hotel.

Next evening when I came home my car was parked on the drive and Krishan was waiting for me on the veranda outside my room.

He stood smiling faintly as I went up to him. His cheek reflected the bronze of the evening sky; he seemed to bloom and glow like a flower—nothing sweet and ordinary, not a rose or a lily, but a dark, rather succulent species that would probably bring you out in a rash if you touched it, or snap its petals on your finger.

"Brother says you will take me to your friend."

"Does he want me to?"

He nodded and smiled with such a look of conspiracy I knew he was lying.

At the time I was in the dark as to what happened and later Giles told me all about it.

In fact, Shankar was strongly against the whole idea, and he had not told Krishan what my note contained because he had no intention of doing anything about it. But he was careless with his things, and had left the note lying on his mantelpiece.

Shankar's own life was an unconsidered mess, and he lived from day to day, one jump ahead of his worries and misfortunes. But for Krishan his purpose was remarkably steady, and he looked to a future when the boy would hold a post in some respectable profession. Now this boy—his beloved but somehow difficult brother—asked for permission to step out of Shankar's dream, a dream he had spun for so long and served so consistently that to depart from it seemed like a betrayal of faith.

"What about your degree at the University?" Shankar said. "If you do this you will not get B.A."

"This is better. Mr. Moate will teach me to type and to read Shakespeare. He promised me he will give me education. Not Indian education," he said with contempt.

"You will not get B.A.," Shankar insisted. "What degree can this man give you?"

"Perhaps," said Krishan, "he will take me back to England and send me to Oxford."

"That is foolish, and if he said it he is lying and wishes to exploit you. To go to Oxford you must get B.A."

"He will take me to England," said Krishan sulkily. His brow had grown sullen and the light had gone out of his eyes. Shankar knew that look, and he felt the pain he always experienced when he had to refuse Krishan something he wanted.

"Did he promise this?" he gently asked.

"He said he would take."

It had, in fact, been hinted at during the long interview on Giles' much-cushioned divan. For Krishan too had had reservations—he had been afraid that he might actually have to work— and, seeking for areas of greed in the boy's nature, Giles had offered him the use of the car, clothes and a vague promise of betterment.

But Shankar shook his head. "You must get your degree."

That evening Krishan went out. He returned home at three in the morning to find Shankar waiting up for him. Shankar's own nature was ascetic and puritanical; he lived a simple, abstemious life and, though emotionally self-indulgent, he was stern with his own senses. He now made the mistake of lecturing Krishan. "Where have you been? You are only a child, and this is no time to come home."

Krishan flung himself down on his charpoy, his upturned face flushed with exhaustion and rage. What he had only half wanted was now something he could not live without. His will pushed against his brother's, sluggish and soft, but with the power of total application and consistency. "What does it matter? Who cares what happens to me? My life has no purpose. I am offered a future by a distinguished man of high position, and out of envy and malice my own brother stands in my way."

"I will consider," said Shankar.

This, however, he did not do. He put the whole question out of his mind, and was aware only of a sore spot in his consciousness, where thought, if thought had been permitted, would have taken place. To think would have been to incur pain and invite perplexity. In making decisions one took risks and only God had the skill to play with lives. Decisions, therefore, were made outside the range of thought, and were subject to accidental phenomena. A star fell . . . a bird dropped dead . . . a Brahman bull passed the door. A letter came. . . .

It was from Dattu, Shankar's second brother, who wanted money to start a business in Calcutta—his fourth experiment in commercial life, the previous three attempts having suffered from overexalted aims. This time he had kept one foot on the ground and proposed to open a shop dispensing Modern Art and Dry Cleaning.

I have a friend [Dattu wrote] who is a genius. His masterpieces reveal the soul of India in all her mystic rhythms. It is our duty to give this greatness to the world.

Dattu had found geniuses before—painters, writers, poets— and Shankar was skeptical about his new discovery, but the end of the letter swayed his mind:

For years now you have squandered on Krishan those benefits that belong to all your brothers. What has he done while we have fended for ourselves? Help me, brother. I trust to your sense of family duty. Only good can come from the pursuance of duty, and your acts will bring you lasting satisfaction.

Yet some residue of doubt must have remained to trouble Shankar. A vague, intuitive apprehension, a half-acknowledged understanding of how Krishan might use his good luck. Or was it Krishan himself who put doubt in his mind when he said in his sly, persuasive way, "But, brother, cannot you trust Mr. Mardellis? He is your friend."

Trust? Trust, in India? Tuberculosis and dysentery are the diseases of the flesh, suspicion the disease of the mind. The obverse side to those ebullient, affectionate natures with their enthusiasms flaring up and burning like fire in straw. Such passionate affirmations must have their spiritual winters, and friendships are forever breaking up and alliances shifting to the crushing traffic in rumors, betrayals and lies. Shankar trusted me, but even he could not escape what was dust in the air and blown ceaselessly about by the four winds. It is unwise in India to mention trust, for it puts the idea of suspicion into the mind.

Chapter Seven

THROUGHOUT THE REST OF THAT WEEK I SAW VERY LITTLE OF the Siegels. On the Thursday and Friday I stayed at the College for lunch, and in the evenings they must have gone out, for they did not appear for dinner.

But on Saturday afternoon a knock came at my door, and there was Fred, with his soft, stooped shoulders, his smile and his worried brow. He came in and nosed around my room, his curiosity as ravenous and undisciplined as Alisulman's. Immediately he began to match his fortunes against mine. What! no air conditioning? Only an old ceiling fan that let out a muffled report on each lethargic revolution. And no refrigerator either! What a dilapidated place they had given me.

He looked at my books and borrowed two; discovered a bundle of Survey maps and borrowed these. What had I been doing, he wanted to know. Elly and he had missed me—you'd think we'd been friends for years. Was that red car on the drive mine? Yes, it was. Talking on, covering his tracks, he arrived at asking if by any chance I was going out that evening? Elly and he had been "invited," so perhaps I wouldn't mind . . . ?

I would have driven fifty miles for five minutes with Helen Siegel so I didn't mind at all.

I walked beside her from the new annex, across the lawn—a creature disconcertingly new, for I had not expected from my barefooted Crow maiden this perfection in terms of another world, this varnish and shine. She wore a dove-gray dress that was tight and short, cut low on her breasts and supported over her shoulders by very thin straps. But she didn't look naked in it; her skin fitted her like a lustrous brown sheath, and was part of her beauty, like the skin of an animal.

She didn't thank me for playing chauffeur, she let Fred do that. She knew instinctively what so many of us never learn: that there are no gifts in life, only exchanges, and that when we take without full payment we sign ourselves into captivity.

My own rewards were quickly rendered. Fred and Helen sat in the back where I could not see her, and Fred talked all the time. However, I did manage to seize a word. Precisely one word.

I said, "What state are you from, Helen?"

"Victoria."

"Her father is a McLeish," said Fred. "You must have heard of the McLeishes."

It was one of those names which in Australia is called "well known." I had heard of it many times and thought of race horses and sheep. Fred went chattering on, elucidating on a distinction that he clearly believed had rubbed off on him. "He has a big property in the Western District. Zey are one of the oldest Victorian families."

I heard more of this later on, for Fred was excessively proud of Helen's family. "Zey are four generations Australian. Zere were four brothers in the beginning who were very wealthy and bought a lot of land. These early settlers are the aristocrats of Australia."

And Helen smiled, saying, "Four generations! Think of that!"

There is something touchingly ridiculous about Australian snobberies. The hard past stands too close . . . the thirst in the desert, failed crops and pasture returning to sand. I could not imagine Helen subscribing to fantasies, or obedient to the provisions of a ready-made identity, and I asked myself if she had married Fred to escape being a McLeish. Though a European of heaven knows how many generations, who could be less of an aristocrat, in that prudish, confident, respectable Australian way, than Fred Siegel?

Fred and his fathers had been persecuted and jailed. Their own misfortunes and other people's wars had made them greedy and corrupt. They had sold their friends and their silver candelabra for a loaf of bread. They were subtle and sly, but they knew a great deal about suffering and they could weep without loss of manhood. They were everything, in fact, that was not McLeish. So to Fred and his fathers Helen turned, little realizing that Fred would take the name of McLeish as a passport to a new life and demand that it should be presented at all frontiers.

Passports loomed large in Fred's life, for he was a refugee, and the one that had come to him at length had looked too brand new to seem adequate. Something was needed, some background for an identity so spare as to attract mistrust and disbelief: money, property, names—even the names of race horses, belonging to brothers and cousins-in-law whom he had never met. A world that was not his, but possessed as an adjunct to his own property, now clothed him with a warmth which, if reluctantly donated, was yet comforting.

Fred was still a boy when he left Germany with his father; it was the year Hitler marched into Austria. His mother was dead, his sister married to an Army officer, later killed at Stalingrad. His father, Johann Siegel, was a student of history who had looked hard at the European situation, and watched it slowly confirming his prophecies. He had not fled from Hitler's Germany because it was abhorrent to him, but because he felt it could not survive. Any month now his son would be pulled into the Army; there would be a war and Germany would lose it. Johann did not want to pass his remaining days in a defeated country.

The year 1945 found Johann dead and Fred in Australia. But the distresses of war passed him by, for he found himself apologetically interned.

Some public protest brewed up over these internments—sheep and goats herded together in one large act of necessary inhumanity—and when they came to be released, some wore a look of martyrdom, Fred amongst them. For who could be more gentle and less disposed to violent underground action than this harmless alien, with his gaiety, his industry—he had spent the five war years studying toward a profession—and his habit of bowing his head over feminine hands?

One feminine hand over which he bowed belonged to Helen's mother. The right hand—brown, freckled, beringed—the left held a cocktail glass, and the scent of a gardenia in her coat lapel mingled with the perfumed oil in Fred's hair. That was later. He was thirty-two, naturalized and with a job in a firm of chemical manufacturers. With charming half-cynical gaiety, he told Mabel McLeish how he and his father had fled from Hitler's Germany, how his father had died a year later and how Australia had interned him during the war.

She telephoned her husband. "I'm bringing him back for the weekend. I felt so sorry for him, and he really is very charming, with wonderful manners and *such* an attractive voice. He wears awful scented hair oil, but that's typically European, and you'll just have to overlook it. Don't *say* anything about it. I wouldn't hurt him for worlds!"

Somewhere, far back, Mabel could claim to a dash of German blood which suddenly became an important element in her nature. She remembered songs she had learned as a child, and sang them to him as they drove the hundred miles home.

> "Sah ein Knab' ein Röslein stehn
> Röslein auf der Heide." . . .

Fred, delighted, sang back to her in a pleasing light baritone.

The headlights of the car opened up the vacant road and the drooping silent gums edged the moon-covered paddocks on either side. Here no wars, no treacheries and no candelabra. And at the big, sprawling bungalow, in a room which contained a pianola, thirty-five racing trophies, four dogs and a billiard table, he met Helen McLeish—a brown, fair-haired, boyish-looking girl in an open shirt and riding breeches.

"Be nice to him, dear," Mabel whispered. "He really is charming and he's had such a tragic life."

But when, three months later, Helen happened to say that

Fred Siegel had asked her to marry him, Mabel was horrified. And Helen, up till then undecided, made up her mind.

I put them down at the Embassy porch. A Sikh doorman in starched turban and scarlet cummerbund opened the car door, and in they walked—Fred with his head reaching forward, pushing his smile before him, and Helen McLeish, taking everything for granted—me, Fred, the Embassy and India.

I found Shankar sitting outside on the roof, talking with two of his friends—Government clerks who lived in the same colony. Rani's grandmother had also come out to enjoy the evening and Rampal and Mira sat together on a charpoy, reading their schoolbooks aloud to each other.

No Krishan, of course, but his absence hung about us like bereavement. Shankar mentioned him only once. It was after his friends had left. Rampal and Mira and the grandmother had gone to bed, and we sat alone with the sky above us full of stars.

"Richard," he said in a low voice, "I have a confession to make. I have been thinking about it all night and the night before. I could not sleep. I lied to you. . . ."

His words filled me with deep uneasiness, but I said lightly, "I expect it was for my own good."

"No, no, you must hear me. I told you that the road to Agra has now been swept away by the monsoon. This is untrue. I told you so that you would give up your desire to go there—but road has been mended. You can drive to Agra now whenever you wish."

Now I wanted to laugh, but he was taking himself so seriously laughter would have offended him. "Shankar," I said, "can't you see that it doesn't matter my not having got stuck on the Agra road on a trip that I didn't take?"

His face only became more tragic. "This doesn't matter—I understand. But it matters that I tell lies to you." He fell silent a moment; then he said in a low voice, "It is terrible when you so love another that even their faults become dear to you, like little children that need your protection and care."

So now we were getting down to the meat of the matter. I felt an irrational twinge of anger. I leaned toward him. "Shankar, if you continually support other people's deficiencies, you weaken them . . . or you turn them into parasites that can only live on your blood. Look at you and your brothers. They know they don't have to lift a finger to help themselves and they never will. And there are thousands of families in India just like yours—millions of lazy, weak young men, living off someone else's energy and brains."

But he only smiled and shook his head. "You and I will never agree on these matters. Our gifts—energy, brains or whatever you like—are not our own, and it is our duty to share them with those who do not have them. We need our parasites, as you call them, to save us from selfishness and pride."

It was after midnight when I left. The dogs were still barking and the gurdwaras still pumping out their prayers. I had enjoyed myself, as I always did with Shankar, but this—though I did not know it—was the end of our friendship, and the last of those long, pleasant evenings sitting on his roof under the stars.

There had been times that night when I had felt uneasy. He had looked at me with an expression that I did not want to analyze. I had had a feeling that at any moment he might confront me with some problem I was not facing, or uncover some hypocrisy I had managed to accommodate within my nature. He made me feel guilty—with the obscure, resentful guilt we feel toward someone who has undertaken a sacrifice on our behalf, or burdened us with too much innocent trust.

Chapter Eight

AGAIN NEXT MORNING FRED WAS AT MY DOOR. WAS I DOING anything? Elly and he were members of the Ashoka swimming club and could take me as their guest. So presently we were driving down Lodi Road, weaving our way through the tongas and the motor scooters.

The pool lay open to the sun, a scoop of blue water slapping and swaying in the palm of the green lawns. Fred and I lay on the grass in the shade of some overhanging bushes, while Helen sat in the sun rubbing oil on her beautiful legs.

I said, "You know, this isn't Australia. Too much tropical sun isn't good for you."

"I keep telling her that," said Fred, and added proudly, "You can't do anything with Elly. She just goes her own way."

"It's all right," she said, "if you're careful." And then lay down, folding her towel as a pillow for the back of her head. The more she took off, the better she looked—the more like herself as though to feel fully alive she needed to put in use every inch of her body. Fred, on the other hand, was decidedly improved by clothes. From throat to navel he was a thick mat of curly black hair, with two patches of nakedness encircling his raspberry nipples. He kept himself covered most of the time in a white toweling robe that exposed only his hairy legs and soft snow-white feet. When he wasn't talking he played a transistor radio and hummed tunelessly to the Indian songs. He seemed to know most of the people who were disposed around the grass, and was constantly sitting up and waving at someone.

Hilton and his wife, Fern, sat with a group of young people on the other side of the pool. Fred waved; they waved back, and Hilton's smile flagged a little as his eyes moved over to mine.

"I just want to have a word with him," said Fred, and off he went, delicately treading the hot grass as if it were gravel.

Suddenly silence; no Fred—just Helen and me. I lay on my belly, she lay on her back, and our bodies, brushed by the soft-lipped air, were disposed in the form of a T of which I was the perpendicular and she the horizontal. Had I shifted nearer I could have dropped my lips upon a sliver of peeled white flesh that opened like a broken seam between the edge of her bathing trunks and her chestnut thigh. I looked at her legs and her ankles and her beautiful, long, narrow feet, and I guessed that she spent a lot of time attending her body—dressing herself, oiling her skin, painting her nails. She was so right for every occasion, as though she looked straight at each advancing moment and gave herself to it in exactly the measure that was asked. Never too little or too much; never an embarrassing excess or a withdrawal into chilly reservation.

She shifted a little and I wondered if she felt my thoughts. I put out my hand and closed my fingers about her ankle. Her skin was silky and hot. I moved it with my fingers, shifting it about on the bone beneath, and it was tight on the bone, but moved with a lissome slide like the pelt on the skull of a dog.

She lifted her head, and held up her hands to make a shade for her eyes. They looked into mine, blanched by the sun, shrinking a little, severe. "What are you doing?"

"Praising your beautiful feet."

She gave a little snort that sounded derisive but covered a moment's nervousness. She told me afterward, "The moment you put your hand on my foot, I said to myself, 'I know this man. I've met him before.'" There had been a friend of her father's—a married man with a reputation for liking young girls. When she was fifteen he had followed her into her bedroom and, coming up behind her, kissed the back of her neck. Two years later she met a young man at a dance given for merchant seamen. Somehow they were different, those two, from the other men she met, and something about them made them seem identical. The silky, calculating touch of the practiced seducer.

"You felt them far away, standing off, getting their effects from sheer dexterity. Like good tennis players. They know just how to land the ball on the back line. And it happens on purpose. Everything happens on purpose. Somehow you don't like it. You say to yourself that a man can't feel when he is so much in control."

How wrong she was! But dexterity, if we have ever achieved it, remains part of our equipment, and drops automatically to hand even when we are fighting for our lives.

She had got my message now, but it had taken her by surprise. Her defense was to be very prim and married.

"There are lots of women who actually enjoy having their feet stroked by strangers." She had rolled right away from me, so that we weren't a T any more, but an open triangle.

"We're not strangers."

"People are strangers when I've only met them twice."

"Four times."

She thought, going back to count. "Three times. That other time we hadn't met."

"But you remember it and that's a kind of meeting. I learned all I need to know about you then. You're beautiful, potentially passionate and shamefully neglected. It's my duty to do something about you."

"Look, Richard . . . if you want to come out with us then don't talk to me again like this, because I don't like it. It's just *silly*. I'm a married woman and there are plenty of girls. . . ."

Fred came back.

"Let's go again next week, shall we?" said Fred. So there we were again the following Sunday. And the next, and the next. Then when the days began to grow cool, we gave up swimming and took to riding instead.

There was a stretch of open land near the riding school—a stony rise scribbled with goat tracks. Indians, who like to glorify humble things, called it a jungle. But there was very little vegetation; acacias, putting out a feathery green, and a few low, rubbishy bushes. It was pleasant up there in the early mornings when the air was fresh and the bushes full of bee eaters and robins. Peasant women walked down the paths, carrying baskets of dung cakes on their heads, and our shy, spoiled ponies pricked their short, neat ears at the dragonflies.

In the afternoon I took them into Connaught Circus, where we looked at the jades and paintings in the antique shops. We visited every mosque and tomb in Delhi. The shadows gathered like honey under the domes, and the sun, breaking back from the marble floors, basted our arms and cheeks with yellow light. Helen liked the gardens more than the tombs themselves. She listened with interest when I told her stories about the Moguls and explained the evolution of the different architectural styles, but when left to herself she wandered away to watch the animals and birds. She sat for an hour on the grass by Humayun's tomb, holding out nuts for the squirrels on her long, flat palms.

The Siegels were the whole of my life at that time, but I was by no means so important to them. Always there were the "invitations," and these became more frequent as people they met at parties asked them to more parties. And so it went on.

I asked her once, "Don't all these parties bore you?"

"No," she said, and looked surprised. Because she lived largely on the surface of events, every occasion was fresh to her and nobody bored her. She would come home from a party delighted about something new she had eaten, the color of somebody's sari or the way they had hung up the lights in the trees. There was an uncalculating honesty in her responses. She was outside the current trends, and didn't even know what it was fashionably thought she ought to feel. She seemed right and wise, like a healthy animal, and as specifically defined, with hard, sharp edges and clear limitations. She never attempted what she could not achieve, never used words whose meaning she could not fully understand, and so was never defeated, never lost.

As for Fred—well, right from the beginning, I underrated Fred. Because we were exploiting each other, and because this was a fact that I knew and he didn't, he seemed always small and manageable—a feeble ant of a man. I barely accorded him an identity of his own, and it took me a while to realize that people liked him. He was gay and he enjoyed himself. Life was a feast and he gobbled every morsel. It was the one quality that Helen and he had in common. Moreover, he liked people—not just some, but everyone; and people in general respond to such generous, unselective appreciation. They like to know that for once they are not being criticized and measured. Fred assessed them, not in their qualities, which were intrinsic, but in their usefulness, which was circumstantial, so that there could be no disgrace in failing to reach the top of his list.

By this system of measurement I qualified as his closest friend, Otto Schlacht coming next as a close runner-up.

I first met Otto at a picnic. . . . Sunday, two cars and lunch at Tughlakabad.

At a quick glance, Otto looked thirty-five, but he was probably nearer fifty. A big, heavily-built man—there was no fat on him, but he was so compact and solid I wondered if he was corseted. He had the anxious, cared-for look of a man who is weighing every ounce of flesh that the years put on him, and the tan of his skin was calculated to the nicest intensity, as though he had put on the sun like make-up, to match his straw-colored hair and aluminum eyes. He was handsome in the Teutonic way, his face constructed on rigid horizontals and perpendiculars, the ears lying snug and close to the head and the eyebrows drawn straight under a flat slab of forehead. Only his mouth curved. It looked rubbery and soft, as though the skin had been peeled away from his lips.

There were children with us that day, the daughters of a

lively Bengali woman named Indra Braden, who had married an American engineer in T.C.M. But Otto took no part in the exploring, the feeding of monkeys and games of hide-and-seek. He stood about looking handsome, superior and bored. Neither did he bother to talk unless you talked to him.

At lunch he sat in the shade, his back against a rock, stuffing slabs of chapatti into his mouth and chewing like a machine. Rarely have I known a presence so cold and slack. His glance was so unlit I hardly realized he was looking at me.

"You are a friend of Giles Moate. Isn't that so?" he said.

"Yes, I know Giles."

He leaned forward and picked up an orange from a dish. It was a slow, deliberate, mechanical action, like the action of chewing the chapatti. He broke the orange in two, then, putting each half to his mouth, sucked it dry.

One of the children ran up and stood holding out her hands. "Please do not throw your rind. Give it to me." A pretty Indian girl, about thirteen, her body thin and unformed but her large eyes looking down with a direct and provocative glance that was fully matured.

"Ah! You want these?" He looked up and fixed her with his eyes. For a moment a glint of greed animated his heavy, immobile face.

"Please. We are feeding them to the monkeys."

He kept his eyes on hers as he gave them up. Then she ran away and he wiped his glistening lips on the back of his hand.

"Where did he get that boy?"

"You mean Giles?"

"I thought it was you who found him."

"He's the younger brother of a friend. He wanted a job and I happened to know that Giles was looking for someone."

"Ah!" He leaned back against the rock and the crenelated shadow of the fort fell across his forehead. Laughing and shouting, the children rushed about feeding orange rinds to the monkeys.

As time passed, I saw more of him. Fred would always include him in any excursion that was not just for the three of us. "We ought to ask Otto. He is a lonely chap."

Otto would have dampened other spirits, but not Fred's. He seemed not to notice Otto's vanity, his lack of generosity, his ill temper. But Helen didn't like him.

"But I know why I don't like him," she told me. "So I put up with him as a penance, because it isn't any reason at all."

"Because he doesn't like you."

"You've got it in one."

"But he does."

"Not as much as he should."

"Not as much as I do."

"No, not nearly as much as you. Or as much as . . ." And then I had to listen to a string of names, all dragged in to exclude me from any unique position in her life.

"Then you won't miss Otto, with all those."

She was right of course, though she had perhaps not guessed the reason. It was simply that at thirty she was too old. Otto preyed upon human flesh, but it had to be tender, moist and tight in the bud.

Chapter Nine

ONE EVENING, WHEN THE SIEGELS WERE OUT AT A PARTY TO which I had not been invited, I dropped in on Giles.

He had rented the top flat of a square concrete building in one of the new colonies, and we sat on the roof under a sky that was still full of light but had drained all its colors down to earth. A dull red blush was shrinking away on Delhi's extended and undistinguished skyline, and overhead in the thin white air kites glided and turned. Across the road in the nulla, Rajasthani women from the building gangs squatted to defecate—vivid splashes of color in their crimson skirts, and a spectacle for the daily nourishment of Giles' aversions.

Friendship in India is not a matter of choice but of fate; otherwise I might not have been there, passing an hour with Giles Percival Moate, ex-Cambridge, ex-B.B.C. and now on a UNESCO assignment that had something to do with teaching English by radio.

Giles was thirty-nine, unmarried, five feet eleven and very thin. He had a narrow face that he made a point of keeping expressionless. His blue eyes were observant and restless—a prowler's eyes. When they regarded you, you could sense him looking over the top of your virtues, into the less seemly back yard of your nature.

The previous summer, while Pamela was up in Mussooru escaping the heat, I had had a brief affair with a Canadian girl, that same young woman who took a carving knife to her father. It was unimportant, but Giles happened to know about it, as he knew, three months later, about Margaret. In fact, the affair with Margaret could hardly have taken place without him. He had a room in one of the hotels in Old Delhi at the time, and we needed somewhere to meet.

I don't think he ever told Pamela, but there was always the happy thought for him that he could if he wanted to, and I am convinced that without knowledge of these little adventures he would have found me totally uninteresting. For my own part, in some curious way they attached me to Giles. It was as though I had stretched a hand outside my marriage into that anarchic world where people live who have no responsibilities. I had put out my hand and encountered his, tugging a little, soliciting— for all men proselytize for their own way of life, even when it becomes abhorrent to them. Pamela loathed him. "I've got no prejudice against queers, but he's awful. What can you see in him?" She could not express her aversion more distinctly and I could appreciate every element that strengthened it, yet I could not bring myself to shake off that ghostly clasp. It was symbolic of a secret and tentative freedom. I will even admit that I enjoyed his company; he had the power of giving me respite from myself. He exhilarated me by asking nothing of my character, just as Shankar wearied me by asking too much.

Giles made no concessions to his friends' personalities or to their interests and, as soon as he had given me a drink and a chair, he expressed aloud those thoughts that had occupied him before I arrived. A dissertation upon the composition of India's soil, based on samples that he claimed to have taken from the adjacent building lots and analyzed down to their basic components.

"Mud, muck and human shit—in three equal portions."

"Muck?"

"Spit, bones, bits of rag, rotten food . . ."

"Surely no food. What are your scavengers doing?"

"They get to it when it's too far gone and then they die. More rotten food for more scavengers."

He stretched out his long, bony legs. His elbows rested on the curved cane arms of his chair—one hand held a gin-and-tonic, the other scratched about in the ebony curls of Krishan's hair. He was wearing a dhoti, a long, hand-woven cotton shirt and a pair of Punjabi slippers stitched with gold thread. Krishan—wearing tailored raw-silk trousers, suède shoes and an American nylon shirt—sat at his feet.

The Indian dress was a new fad for Giles, but it didn't surprise me. His responses were never halfhearted, and he liked India. It suited him to live in a country where virtue has never been organized into a social force, and where eccentricity can blossom without reproof.

In Old Delhi, on the maidan before the Red Fort, you may see a naked sannyasi lying on his belly in the dust with a pebble in his outstretched hand; up he gets, takes a step and down he lies—measuring his length to Benares, and the best of all possible funeral pyres. In the public streets men wash, defecate, masturbate, pray, go into trances, stand on their heads, go mad—even die—without attracting much curiosity or stirring any public indignation. Giles felt relaxed in this climate of unrestrained individualism and permitted excesses. Here, if anywhere, he was safe from the improvers he detested; and though he professed to loathe India, his nature needed to feel disgust as it needed to feel free. Of all the Europeans I knew in Delhi, he was the most likely to remain. I could imagine him finishing his days in an ashram—a mad old man, who had reduced his world to a vegetarian diet, a charpoy and a spinning wheel.

"Dear boy, Richard's glass is empty. Get him another tot, there's a good child."

But Krishan knew his place, which was with the masters, not the servants, and, turning his head, shouted for the bearer. He too had his glass of gin, which he took in small greedy sips, sucking up the ice, rolling it around in his mouth and spitting it back again into his glass. He was putting on weight, and his plump throat was ringed with violet creases. I wondered if he was getting anything worth while from his new life—apart from good food and soft living. Giles could talk if he wanted to; he was intelligent and widely read. If Krishan were so inclined, there was something to be got out of him.

But there he was, sitting cross-legged on his spongy little bottom, spitting the ice into his glass and drawing it back again through his succulent lips.

I said, "How's the typing going, Krishan?"

He looked up—or, rather, half looked up, for he never fully opened his eyes—and his insouciant, polished gaze turned to Giles. "How is my typing going?"

"As bad as can be." He gestured with his hand. "Look, there goes another."

A woman, carrying her brass jar, crossed the road into the adjacent lot and squatted down, screened by her long crimson skirts.

"My dear fellow, just imagine the future. . . . Next year, the year after. . . . Look at that! Look at that!"

All about us in the growing colony were houses in various stages of construction. Houses needing only a roof or a gate, piles of bricks where houses would soon begin, foundations two feet high where work had stopped because the money had run out. Said Giles, "The number of shit fields is daily shrinking. That's something the agents don't warn you about. I picked this place because of all the vacant plots, and congratulated myself on having dispensed with neighbors, wireless sets and yelling kids. It never occurred to me what a bit of open land might mean. Now I sit here breathing the scented air, and pray for an eruption of little houses."

I said to Krishan, "When did you last see Shankar?"

He shrugged his shoulders. "Yesterday, the day before. I do not remember. He has gone to Calcutta to help brother."

"Have you ever really considered this question? Imagine the whole of India, like a map, spread out before you. . . . An enormous tract of land to which every day four hundred and fifty million human beings make their individual contributions."

"There are lavatories."

"Filthy, irreligious inventions fouled by other people. . . . My dear fellow, you might just as well say there are cases of constipation. Think of the dysentery. According to a recent WHO survey in a south Indian village, an estimated ninety-eight per cent of the population suffers from amoebic dysentery. You can't put me right on these statistics, I've studied them closely. And what do you think is going to happen when in twenty years' time the population doubles? Think of it! Nine hundred million individual piles of excrement. It won't be safe to set foot out of doors. To say nothing of the shitting animals—the cows and buffaloes, dogs and pigs."

"And the birds," said Krishan, laughing as a crow, flying over the roof top, left a white splash on the pink cement balustrade.

"Listen to the little lamb! And the *birds*." And, bending down, he cuddled the boy's round cheeks in the palms of his hands and poured down into his upturned face a look of expectant and unaffectionate lust.

I put down my glass. "I'm off."

"He's off. Krishan, see Richard out. Remember he's your benefactor."

"No," I said, *"you* see me out."

But just then another visitor arrived, his blond head pushing up from the stairs that led onto the roof, and I found myself shaking the brown, well-tended hand of Otto Schlacht. He nodded, but did not bother to change his expression. It occurred to me that he avoided smiling for fear of putting lines in his waxy cheeks.

"You're coming to my housewarming," said Giles, as we went down the stairs.

"Aren't you a bit late for housewarming?"

"I've been busy domesticating that little pussy. Have to teach him to use his sand tray."

The murmur of Otto's voice sneaked down the stairs. We

reached the hall, and I saw Giles' face grow blank as he strained to listen.

"Does he see his brother, Giles?"

"He *says* he does. But he's such a bloody little liar. I don't know what he gets up to. I'm out all day."

"See that he does. You know in India these family ties. . . ."

"Just a minute." And he whisked around and darted off up the stairs. I waited, listening to the dying gurgle of Krishan's laughter.

Then silence. But Giles did not come back, so after a moment I left, returning to the hotel to sit on the lawn and hear all about the party from Helen and Fred. They had met that attractive Kashmiri, and had I noticed that Kashmiris had green eyes? Indra had said that Rome was dirty; wasn't that funny when you came to think of it? Coming home they had passed a procession, and was it a wedding, did I suppose, with a man completely hidden in marigold garlands that hung down in a sort of veil over his face? He was riding along on a white horse and a small boy sat up in front of him.

I was not, as it might sound, totally occupied in driving the Siegels around Delhi and contemplating Helen's unstudied charms. I did have work to do.

The alternative site for the new College building had come up for open discussion, and on top of lectures we had been subjected to a wearisome amount of Ministerial visiting. Then suddenly the seminar at Agra, which had been several times postponed, was revived, and Prasad dispatched me off for four days. Usually I enjoyed a trip to Agra, a city which contains buildings of such beauty that you can never confront them—not for the hundredth time—without surprise. But this time I was leaving my playmates behind, and as I got into my car early on a Monday morning I had an odd sense of loss, more poignant than I had ever expected. Up till now I had taken the days for granted; they had slipped casually by, and it wasn't till later that I recognized this as one of the fine, happy periods of my life.

Alisulman ran out to the gate waving a letter from Pamela. I had written only twice in the past month and knew I could count on a sizable dossier of reproaches. As it was six-thirty, the letter could hardly have come by the morning post and I wondered how long it had been lying around in the dust on Agawalla's desk. I put it, unopened, into my pocket.

Delhi was only just beginning to stir and here and there the morning fires had been lit. Thin columns of smoke leaned in the air and, spilling out, met with one another to form a blue transparent shield over the face of the earth. Milkmen cycled along with their big cans, one on either side of the handle bars, and India's beautiful humpbacked cattle flicked their tufted tails at the flies.

Outside Delhi there was still a lot of water lying about and the road was in bad shape, the center breaking up into potholes and the sides eaten away by the rains. Sometimes it slipped into a shallow film of water: then, just beyond Palwal, it disappeared altogether, diving into a broad, shallow lake.

I pulled up and, leaning on the wheel, thought of Shankar— of bubbles and balls of lead, of grains of sand and mountains far away. Trees on the other side of the water looked hazy, like a mirage, and egret stood about with their heads bunched into their snowy shoulders. Workmen who had been banking up the road splashed toward me. They wore their dhotis tucked up above their brown, woody knees and lifted their shovels from the mud to show me the water level. Very shallow, they said; they would push me over. Halfway across they shoved me into a ditch and abandoned me, till I shouted and waved a bundle of rupee notes. They turned and came splashing back, and again I thought of Shankar, who had drained these fields and rebuilt the road, making me a sacrifice to his need for excessive self-abnegation.

On dry land the car would not start and it took me half an hour to get it going. Then a puncture at Vrindaban, Krishan's birthplace, with its scores of squalid temples and its home for old cows. A host of villagers erupted out of the fields like the resurrecting dead, touched the wheels, held the tools, wanted payment. I made Agra in the evening, stripped of my small change and feeling bad-tempered.

The hotel, with its big, bird-filled garden and its lofty rooms, looked wistfully out from years that had barely watched the century turn over. Once you get out of New Delhi, India still sleeps in its old skin. The bearers wore starched turbans and crimson sashes braided with tarnished gold; King George V looked down from a frame on the wall. I went to my room through a long, sallow corridor, where the heads of tigers snarled from wooden shields. I was filthy and looking forward to a bath.

But there was no hot water, and as darkness fell the electricity failed. In the bar, bearers hurried about, shouting at one another and carrying kerosene lamps; and here I spent an hour with an Englishman who was down in Agra for the weekend but worked in timber farther north. He had been in India for forty years. He had seen all the changes.

"I like it better now. It's more friendly. You can put your feet up. Mind you," he added, "things are going down the drain. But that's the way they want it. It isn't our business any more."

His name was Thompson and he wasn't a bad chap, though obviously on the edge of being a drunk. Thick red unhealthy blood just under the skin, and features, never too fine, that were clotting up together. He talked too much, jumping quickly into pauses in the conversation as though they frightened him. He told me that he lived alone. His wife had left India years ago and was bringing up their children in England.

Now he exorcised his loneliness with evenings in hotel bars or in his district club, which had not changed in the forty years he had been there, only pursued, unarrested, its slow course of disintegration. I could imagine it, for I had seen many such places during my six months in the U.P. Decaying pampas grass in broken jars; the upholstery bursting out of the chairs, and the sparrows nesting behind the photograph of the old Rajah with his 1920 polo team.

"Of course he doesn't play now. He's eighty-six. But I remember him whacking that ball about when he was sixty. Best string of polo ponies in the Punjab. There was a little white mare, Nur Jehan. . . . He brought her down from Peshawar. When you get up there, there's a strong strain of Arab blood. . . ."

Next morning I lectured to the trainees in the College, and afterward joined a discussion group. I stayed for lunch and we sat at long trestle tables and talked about the power and virtue of India, and the materialism of the declining West. Looking along the table at the dirty frayed collars and the hands, dripping from fingertips to wrist in yellow ghee, I remembered Shankar and his Agra road. And in one of the moods of revulsion that sometimes seized me, I thought what a mess India was—a greasy, grubby physical mess, and a soggy, sentimental intellectual mess. A land of sugar-coated putrefaction; where two lies are better than one truth, and everything is excessive—or nothing at all. And I thought that in my heaven there would be prizes for restraint and rewards for symmetry.

Later that afternoon I drove through the wide cantonment streets to the Taj Mahal. Here, in the green garden that was itself a protest against Hindu confusion, the squirrels and birds hopped up to the mallee and took nuts from his hand. A crowd of schoolgirls walked along the canal from the main gate, their long Punjabi jackets glowing in India's brilliant primary colors, and ahead that most beautiful of all memorials tipped its resplendent image into the water.

I opened Pamela's letter. Its sentiments were familiar and my old protagonists.

I've been rereading your last letter. There aren't any others to read, so I go back to that one. It's beginning to look very old, and I say to myself that you are no longer the person who wrote it. Things have happened to you that I don't know about—things that have changed you, even minutely. You have met new people . . . perhaps you have fallen in love. In any case, you are not the person I used to know, and this makes me feel very lonely.

Don't you understand that it was a difficult decision for me, staying here? I would have thought you might have helped me through it by writing at least once a week. Even lies. That at least would have been kind. Years ago you would have written every day, and once a week doesn't seem too much to expect. Can't you imagine what I might be thinking, waiting here? You know my tendency to depression, particularly when I am alone, but I suppose that only worries you when you have to watch it and it spoils your pleasure.

I expect you're right about the cats, and you're right too in saying that I never know where to stop, but how *can* you stop when it comes to misery and suffering? That's the whole reason why I don't want to come back to India.

You astonish me. You even frighten me at times. This is your work. People pay you to do it. Every day you are forced to look these dreadful facts in the face, and you don't seem to care. You don't even believe in what you're doing. And you *enjoy* yourself. I like living in India, you say, in that casual way, just as you might say I like Monte Carlo, or Venice, or St. Moritz. . . .

I put the letter away. It would be easy to answer, for it had made me angry.

That night in the bar I listened again to Thompson's voice— flat and colorless, like a beggar's whine. He bored me now, but still I sat and listened. I was not sure what it was about him that was rather pitiful. Because what he was now had been inevitable forty years ago; there had been no hope of escape; and so he seemed like a victim—a human sacrifice? Then he had been young and fresh, with ideas of his own and features that were clean-cut and defined; now he was scraped and polished by the gritty frictions of a society that is utterly self-confident and makes no concessions.

Suddenly, on Friday morning, my fourth day in Agra, I felt I could not bear to spend another hour away from Helen. It was the day of Giles' party and I had my last lecture in the morning at ten-thirty. As soon as it was over I started out.

Every bullock cart and bicycle in India stood in my way; then the Palwal water, just as much and just as far. I got to Delhi at five and Alisulman greeted me joyfully as though I had been away for half a year. Soni's grandchildren fluttered about in their twirling dopattas, and the first swallows down from the hills skimmed the water on the lawn.

I went to my room and on the dressing table was a letter from Pamela.

. . . Please forgive me.

. . . I don't know what got into me.

. . . I was going through one of my depressions and I suppose I took it out on you. Darling, you are like a wall on which I scribble my prayers, and all the dirty words I can think of too. Please try to understand. . . .

Alisulman knocked on the door and handed me a note.

Please, Dick, can you take Elly to the party? I've got a stinking cold and I can't go. FRED

Chapter Ten

I KNOCKED.

"Who is zat?"

"It's Dick."

"Dick. . . . Come in. Come in."

He was sitting up in bed wearing a pair of pink pajamas with a large black F embroidered on the pocket. In his hand he held a paper handkerchief into which he dropped a shining, swollen nose. When he lifted his head—which, with a great effort, was done—his face looked white and folded in leathery jowls, as though the grip he had on his own flesh had slipped and let go. "Don't come near me, Dick," he moaned. "I've got a stinging cold."

The paper handkerchief dropped. He clawed blindly in a box and pulled out another. The bed was littered with balls of damp paper; the sheets too looked damp and sick, like their occupant. Pulling them up to his neck, he sank into them, like a buffalo into its wallow. He really looked frightful, and there was a kind of moral frightfulness about him too, that repelled me. I felt a subtle insult in seeing him divested of his physical pride, as though something common to us both had been degraded.

"I did want to go to siz bardy," he moaned. "I don't expect he'll ever ask us again."

I could hardly believe my ears. I sat on the end of the bed. "Do you mean that because you're sick and can't go, he won't ever ask you again? And even if he doesn't, do you really care?"

"You vant to keep on the right side of Giles. He's very touchy. He would make a bad enemy."

Well, that was true enough.

"At any rate, Dick, you can take Elly."

Helen came out of the bathroom carrying a bottle of aspirin.

"I've told you, Fred, I don't want to go. Hullo, Dick." Her eyes barely touched mine. She went to the dressing table and picked up a glass. "How was Agra?"

"You two have spoiled me," I said. "I can't enjoy myself any more without you."

Fred mustered his strength to sit up. "You hear zat, Elly. Dick can take you, darling."

"But I don't want to go."

I said nothing. I just watched her and wanted her as never before. And it wasn't only because now at last after all these weeks Fred was out of the way. Something had happened during my absence from Delhi; a feeling that had once been small and controlled, more like a plan than an emotion, had suddenly grown urgent and obstreperous. And all, as it were, in secret, when my back was turned.

She knew, of course, and I felt her will straining against mine.

She wasn't indifferent; she felt my eyes and answered them with a response she couldn't hide—a brightness, a shine—but she liked the feel of solid ground under her feet and knew that half the suffering in life follows a thoughtless plunge into mysteries. She knew something that Pamela had never learned, that it doesn't matter what you do providing you know exactly what you are doing.

Fred was still arguing away. "But, Elly, why?"

"You're sick."

"I've told you I just want to sleep."

"I'm not in the mood."

He became quite upset and now it turned out that a great deal was at stake. Otto had just come back from a trip to Orissa, and if Elly could manage to have a chat with Otto, the supply of duty-free Scotch that had been suspended while he was away could be made to flow again. X might be there—that chap from the Ministry—and if Elly could be nice to him, Singapore, with all its cameras and cars, might loom up out of the rather unpromising fog into which it had receded. For the past three months Fred had been baiting lines and hanging them out in New Delhi's fruitful waters. It was not only likely but practically certain that at Giles' party the floats would be bobbing up and down, and with nobody there to reel in the fish would get away.

For the first time since I had known her, Helen looked angry. I think she had never before looked critically at Fred, and I hadn't been able to keep back a smile. She unscrewed the top of the aspirin bottle and tipped two tablets into her hand. "Here you are," she said coldly.

Even taking aspirin was worse for Fred than for the rest of us.

He could hardly get them down and sloppily gulped a glass of water. Lying back, he pulled up the sheets, as though seeing himself as a corpse that needed to be covered. "Vat do you want to stay here for, breazing all my germs? You will get zis cold and then just when I am getting better, I will catch it back again. Like zat it will just go on and on and I shall get one stinging cold after another."

And that, of course, decided the matter.

But the fact remained that she had been pushed off by Fred, and when we set off about an hour later her face was still tight and unrejoicing. As near sulky as I had ever seen it. So I talked in my usual way, telling her about Agra and the seminar. Then she relaxed a little and I saw her make the decision to enjoy herself. She smiled when I told her about the workmen on the Agra road pushing me into a ditch, and when I turned to look at her, her eyes met mine with that frank, adolescent look, an exchange between jolly good friends, that left the world of passion unadmitted.

Then we were up on Giles' roof with the kites stitching the sky overhead and our old relationship unimpaired.

"There," said Giles, "you have our local shopping center. And over there our Sikh temple, fitted out with a loudspeaker so you can hear the services in bed. We have had five nonstop, forty-eight-hour services during the past month. They *knew* I was coming. . . ."

It was all deceptively romantic at that hour, with the smoke from the dung fires slipping down into that much-discussed nulla. Here and there a dome showed, suspended above the ground mist—or a minaret, wistfully stating that the past had been beautiful. The roads spun and sparkled with bicycle wheels as New Delhi pedaled home: clerks and peons, dhobis with bundles of washing on their handle bars—the white-clad, flapping and wobbling, perpetually talkative cyclists of India. Beyond the railway line, the huts that had been a village when this was open land huddled in a haze of smoke, and the heavy black shapes of buffalo lumbered home to their night quarters in the Afghan tombs.

"Isn't it typical . . . saving your own soul at the expense of everyone else's health and sanity. Like that marvelous Hindu cleanliness, doing your little bit out in the bush for someone else to tread in. I don't mind. I'm flowing with India. Helen, do you flow with India?"

"I suppose I flow with everything. I'm not a fighter, Giles."

He peered at her with his close-set, predatory blue eyes—searching for hypocrisy, and finding none. "What do you do when you are confronted with something you don't like? Something really intolerably awful."

She thought for a moment. "I go somewhere else."

"But where, in India, Helen, can one *go?*"

Inside, Indians of artistic bent, and some more or less off-color Europeans, done up in raw silk and uneasily converted saris, reclined about on the thick cane furniture, amongst glass-topped tables, black Gwalior pottery and painted clay toys.

Helen knew more people than I did, and someone grabbed her hands and pulled her away. I took a drink from a tray and handed it to her over the muscular brown shoulders of Fern Chase.

"Well, look who's *here!*" Fern's sudden, high-spirited turn nearly knocked the glass from my hand. "Oh gosh! Clumsy me!

Where have you *been*, Richard? We haven't seen you for ages. Hilton, isn't it ages since we saw Richard?" But Hilton, who looked on every party as work, was talking with solemn fervor to an Indian from the Ministry of Education.

"It's my belief that for these technological programs to be truly meaningful . . ."

Fern was a chunky blonde with a blunt, rubbed-up profile and wide mouth. You wondered why she wasn't pretty. Her face looked familiar at first sight, as though it had been stamped out from a pattern too often used, like one of those composite portraits made up from the features of half a dozen beautiful women, with beauty lost somewhere along the way.

"Isn't that one of the wonderful things about India, Richard? Have you ever thought how many things in this room are *handmade!* The rugs . . . the dishes, the drapes! That cute little horse. . . . Giles!" She began to shout for Giles, who was across the room talking about a picture he had just bought from the precious young Bengali who had painted it—oxen, village women, wells—an urban young man, riding the current village wave. "Giles, will you tell me where you got that cute little horse? Oh dash! Oh gosh! He can't hear. Richard, do you know where he got that horse? I sure would like a horse like that."

I found myself being dragged away to look at a black pottery beast with a neck like a giraffe and high, pricked-up ears. Indeed, perhaps a giraffe—except that India knows not of giraffes.

"Perhaps it's a mule," said Fern, doubting too.

Krishan handed drinks about with the air of a host, not of a servant. He must have taken half the afternoon to dress. Such ebony waves, kicking up into such little curls! And what creases in those tight cream pants! He wore his shirt open at the neck, and his round throat was printed at the base with smutty blue indentations, like a strangler's fingerprints. He sidled past Otto Schlacht, and I saw the German, who had been talking to a Swedish girl, stand quiet and still, like an animal that has caught a scent in the air.

I looked for Helen but Indra Braden was introducing her to a tall Indian with a handsome, pock-marked face. So I let her go, deciding that nothing important ever happens at parties, and allowing the smoke, the noise, the inanities to cover my sharper feelings like a fall of snow.

"Darling, I love you for that!" Ram Chandra cried. Love, like God, is everywhere. And neither would I pay my respects to God with a glass of Scotch in one hand and Fern Chase hanging on the other.

But I had left the hotel that night with the sense of entering into a unique occasion, so that for an hour or two everyone seemed to be wearing their best qualities. The dark looked more vivid, the fair more fine and frail; everyone seemed extraordinarily witty and gay. And Helen . . . Well, she was her best for me, and every time I looked at her there she was, with all the lights in her house lit up, so that I felt quite sure of her.

More people arrived, and Giles ordered us back onto the roof, which now hung up above the darkened ground, the squalid shacks and steaming dung fires. Cement balustrades had been strung together with garlands of colored lights, and the sky was our element, lending us, as though for our personal use, its stars, its silence, its immensities.

Giles, for tonight at least, had escaped his disgusts, and India had been reduced to excellent hot curry, some lively young men and beautiful girls, and ninety-six yards or so of gorgeous Benares silk—green, peacock blue, orange and purple—bordered with bands of gold thread.

Around midnight Krishan played the tabla on the roof. A yellow bedspread had been put down in front of some potted oleanders. He sat cross-legged, with a light on his face, and his hands were like brown spiders dancing on the tabla skins.

"Ugh! Ugh! Ah! . . . Ugh!" His Indian audience nodded their approval, grunted or, closing their eyes, wagged their heads in rapture from side to side.

"Ta . . . ta . . . ta. Taaaaaaa ta . . . taa . . . taaaaa."

He called his rhythm out, then paused to look at the sky, as though waiting for far-off stars to issue celestial instructions—a figure exclusive and remote, who seemed uniquely admitted to the halls of sound. Then his supple hands, at the call of ever more stringent directives, danced, galloped, took flight, blurred by their own speed, like a hummingbird's wings.

What a little showman! I thought. What an old, old child! The rhythm seized his body and flung it from side to side. His tongue showed red and wet between his panting lips, like the flesh of a fruit glimpsed through a split in the skin.

"Ta . . . ta . . . taaaaaaaa. Ta . . . ta . . . taa."

"Ugh! Ah! Ugh! Ugh!"

"I say, he's terrific, isn't he?"

"*Ausserordentlich! Wunderschön!*"

"What a bloody frightful language!" said Giles in a high, piercing voice. "There's hardly a word that's strong enough to stand on its own. They're all so soft and soggy they have to flop around and lean on one another."

We left around twelve-thirty. The tabla concert was over then and Giles not to be found.

"Perhaps he's downstairs," I said to Helen. "Let's go and see."

When we got to the bottom of the stairs that led down from the roof, Otto lurched up the passage below and stood gripping the banisters, swaying about, his eyes glazed with drink and his drooping, rubbery mouth all wet and neglected.

"Helen . . . ," he muttered, his intelligence rising to the challenge of a passing face, and then sliding back, like a frog into a pond.

Farther down the passage the door to Giles' bedroom stood half open. Krishan knelt on the bed, his chin tucked in his neck, and his long lashes hanging down over just a slit of eye—a venomous black and white gleam. Giles stood over him, leaning down and saying something in a low voice. His face as I had never seen it before, with its features looking broken and displaced.

Once outside I forgot them. In any case I had no wish to think too much about what was going on in that house and how Krishan was treating his new circumstances.

The prayers from the gurdwara on the other side of the nulla ebbed and flowed into the silence like a tide. I had left the car a little down the road near one of the few trees that had survived from an avenue planted when the first houses were built in the colony. We walked toward it in silence, passing a lean white cow, plucking some bushes over a garden gate.

I didn't start the engine, but sat with my hands on the wheel. I said, "Helen, I haven't got time to beat about the bush."

"Dick . . . I wish you wouldn't."

A street lamp, barely brighter than candlelight, showed her

sitting beside me, looking straight before her with level, wide-open eyes. I told her then that I loved her and wanted her. I knew that she pinned words sternly to their barest meanings, so I told her in bleak, unequivocal phrases, carefully trimmed of exaggerated claims.

I saw her face grow soft and her lips sweeten. I put out my hand and covered her wrist. I said, "You have the most beautiful wrists. Everything about you moves me so much."

Nothing for a moment . . . only that faraway boom of amplified prayers. Then she said, "If you're suggesting that we have an affair, how are you proposing that we go about it?"

"I haven't thought how we would go about it. If you feel as I do, then it will just take place."

"Aren't you forgetting something?"

"No, I don't think I'm forgetting anything. Pamela is on the other side of the world. She doesn't even know you exist." Like all words that have been used too often, they seemed to have lost their virtue. I wished there were others that I could use now for the first time, but could not find them.

I moved my hand up her arm and she swayed toward me. The movement was so slight I knew her will was not behind it, but it made my heart turn. Then she smiled, a tight, ironic, private smile that excluded me. I tried to share it, but could see no cause for irony between us.

She said, "And I suppose he doesn't matter."

He? He? For a moment I couldn't think who she was talking about. Could she mean Fred? There seemed to be no one else, so she must mean Fred. And indeed I had thought that he didn't matter. Or, rather, I hadn't thought of him at all. I couldn't believe that she had any affection for him or owed him any loyalty. The fact of their being married had some explanation in the past. I didn't want to know it. And now this marriage seemed such a waste of Helen I had mentally annulled it.

I said, "Of course not. Everyone matters. Pamela matters too. But she's not here."

"But Fred is. . . ."

Then she said, "Of course I could always ring you up at your work on days when he was working late. Then you could rush back on some pretext or other and we could grab half an hour. Or sometimes when we were asked out I could say I had a headache, except that I very rarely do get headaches. But he might get more colds—he gets a lot of colds. And then I could sneak over to your room." She broke off. "I've never done that before in my life and if I ever begin it will be with someone I don't care about, not with someone I do."

"That's an odd thing to say."

"But isn't that what all men feel? Going off and having their affairs and saying it doesn't matter? I think they're right. Something that isn't important can't have any effect on something that is. It's when you have to choose between two important things— that's when you're in trouble."

Put like that it seemed quite impossible, and clearly this was not for my girl of the sharp lines and the short, noonday shadow. But I sensed her body, warm and excited beside me. Yearning, eager, hot and impatient of those rational restrictions upon love that take everything into account except love itself. There was one moment, breathless and trembling, when I felt her bones bending like green twigs and her breasts crushing soft against my shirt. No thoughts, no words, only hands, lips, cheeks and the exciting smell of a skin that puts out its odor like a hungry demand.

But the moment had been forced and when she could think she resented it. Then she was fighting me off and had gone hard and spiky with enmity. "Please! Don't touch me. Take me home. . . ."

So I drove her home. And I didn't touch her again. But I talked—about what I felt, which was different now, pushed to the point of pain by frustration. About what I believed she felt. And these feelings—passion, tenderness—had a right to express themselves, an irrefutable claim. Of course there was always a price, but what do we expect for nothing?

Once a vision of the price rose before me—the low, furrowed brow, the big pushing smile. And all that went with it—the exaggerated physical miseries, the greedy little plans. And for a moment the whole situation seemed ludicrous.

Even so, I talked without resentment, or expectation, pitching my words at a future that lay outside our present definitions. I had a feeling that Helen could see into it and allowed her the right to direct it. I was beginning to feel a kind of superstitious reverence for her, as though her very limitations failed to confine her, but were rather the pared-down essential expression of a rich and subtle nature, as a mere phrase, tested by time and a million million devotees, may sum up an obscure philosophy.

All in a matter of moments she had taken hold of my love . . . and what had it been? Curiosity . . . desire . . . a craving to possess and explore her body. And enriched it with gravity and a whole new load of sensation. Some of that gravity must have colored my words, so that I spoke with a simple honesty that moved her. She shook her head and said in a distressed voice, "Please, Dick, don't talk. I know that. . . . I know all that. Don't say any more."

So then I drove on in silence, in spite of it all triumphantly happy.

Chapter Eleven

But during the next few days I was faced with the fact that Helen was slowly drifting out of my life.

She warned me as we said good night. "I don't expect we'll be seeing so much of you. The car's arrived. Fred got the papers today."

And I retorted, "I won't be useful any more so he won't have to bother with me."

She said, "And now you won't have to bother with him either, will you?" Which made me angry, because it was true, and because I didn't like sharing Fred's less salubrious qualities. Perhaps it was her way of establishing an emotion between us, less explosive than longing and more comfortable than regret.

In any case it was the end. The end of that odd night with its whispers of impending devastation, and the end of an epoch of my life. A clear-skied time with every day looking alike, so that you could shuffle them up and rearrange them into just the same lighthearted story. The same sunshine and blue cloud-piled skies; the same rosy, blushing tombs—and picnics, and ponies cantering over the broken, goat-trodden ground—and Otto's Scotch in the evening out on the lawn.

Next day, there on the drive, was a spanking-new pale-blue Mercedes, standing among the emerald-green lawns like a car in a show. Fred was so excited you'd think he'd given birth to it, and I'd hardly returned from the College before there he was, knocking on my door—begging me to come, to look, to admire.

But it was as a piece of potential merchandise that it principally charmed him. "Zer is a radio, you see." He turned a knob. "I thought I'd better put one in. The Indians are mad about them. They like all the trimmings. Next time I am going to have those sort of covers like leopard skin. I would like to put in a cocktail bar, but zat costs a lot of money. What do you think, Dick? Ruplal thinks I ought to clear five hundred pounds. And that is *nozing* to what I can make on a Cadillac. They are *mad* about Cadillacs in New Delhi. It is the biggest status symbol. You are *nozing* if you haven't got a Cadillac."

"Where are you going to pick up a Cadillac?"

He was still hoping for that trip to Singapore. There was this conference in January—he was working away at it. Next week he was going to take Sir Malcolm to dinner at that good Indian place in Connaught Circus.

I started saying that a Cadillac in Singapore, if he could lay his hands on one, would cost him as much as it would in New Delhi, but he didn't want to hear. It wasn't greed that lit up his eyes and sent his brain churning out its little plans. It was the delight of getting something for nothing. Money tainted with work never pleased him so well, just as leave that was owed to him never delighted him like a trip he had wangled out of the Ministry.

After that day I saw less and less of them. It was not an abrupt end, but a slow trailing away. Almost every evening they were out in the new car, shopping in New Delhi or visiting friends. Then one day I happened to mention to Ram Chandra that I hadn't seen them about and he told me that they were down in Rajasthan. Fred had not even bothered to say goodbye.

We were almost into winter now, and the mornings were cold. The bearers put on short knitted pullovers that reached the bottom rib and allowed the shirttails to flow beneath. Agawalla had a long, wide-skirted gray coat with a white pin stripe and upstanding collar. All below and above remained as before, except that the cold drove his feet into shoes. The mallees knelt by the flower beds with blankets over their shoulders and their precious heads wound up in lengths of rag, to protect the semen which, along with his brains, every Indian male keeps in his skull.

It was the beginning of Delhi's "season," and three months of the most perfect weather in the world, spicy and chill; crystal sunshine breaking down out of a cloudless sky that rises in sliding tones from silver to purest blue. Soon the tourists would be pouring in to fill up the hotels and to dash off for Agra and Udaipur.

The roads had dried out and the Jumna, that most vague and dissatisfied river, had slid back through swamps and creeks into the course it had chosen for the winter. Flood victims, who had come into Delhi from their inundated villages, abandoned their rag and tin settlements on the maidan outside the Red Fort, piled up their bullock carts and trudged back to their ravaged homes. While they were there, they had provided subject matter for newspaper editorials and inspired a rash of amateur theatrical productions, sponsored by the wives of Ministers and energetic American matrons, who had lent their children to be fairies and bunny rabbits. Now they were gone, the crimson head shawls and silver ornaments, the creaking carts and the slow-stepping bullocks receding from the consciousness of Government and people.

They presented a typical Indian problem. For the Jumna, like Hindu thought and religion, is illusive of definition. Here for the purposes of one argument, there for another. Move the villages, even supposing you could, move the people, and the Jumna, as likely as not, would move too. And in the meantime, year after year, the long pitiful trails of refugees. Disaster, starvation, death. It was the sort of problem that Indians sometimes stared at, and even discussed. But usually, in the end, they looked the other way.

Prasad, conscious of his position, stared harder than most. "We will do a survey," he said, "to see how often these people are flooded out."

"With what object?" I asked.

"With the object," said Prasad, "of gathering some facts. It will be an interesting subject for our research team."

"And how will we use these facts?"

"Facts," he gently told me, "have a virtue of their own. The Western world is always wanting to put them to work. Westerners are hypnotized by the idea of physical action. They see no value in quiescence and contemplation. In Lucknow," he went on, "there lives a holy man, and when I am in that place I go to visit him. In winter that man takes off all his clothes and sits naked. In summer he puts on a great quilted coat that is as thick as four eiderdowns. He has not taken a bath or cut his hair for five years. He never leaves the place where he is even to relieve himself, but sits amongst the waste of his body. His face is calm, he feels no discomfort. The rats crawl upon him and eat his nails. He does not feel them and his mind is full of wise and serene thoughts."

"I would like to visit him."

"I do not think that will be possible," said Prasad, with a severe little frown. "He speaks only with a few privileged ones whom he has known for a long time. You would not like to visit him, Mr. Mardellis, the smell is very overpowering. Even I, who am used to him, find it necessary to keep a scented handkerchief pressed to my mouth."

"So holiness smells. . . . I always thought it might. Doesn't he mind about the handkerchief?"

"He is above all that sort of minding."

"Mr. Prasad, the fact of your doing a research program in these Jumna villages does imply that people are in trouble and that your ultimate object is to help them. This object may be located a long way away in time, perhaps in the next century, but it does seem to me to exist."

"We are all half Westerners now," Prasad said. "This has been brought about by such men as Gandhi and Nehru, whose leadership we all follow. Gandhi was a great admirer of the Christian Bible, which is full of action and social welfare, and we have come to believe that these activities are necessary to our country. But action, Mr. Mardellis, can be a very dissipating force. We waste ourselves in the violence of movement. In India we have our own strength, and we must not lose it in this sudden frenzy of rushing about that has overtaken us. When there is a great deal to be endured, it is more important to build up powers of endurance."

We were particularly busy at the College just then. Exams were coming up, then holidays, when Prasad and I would go down to Madhya Pradesh. Lectures finished at four and most of the staff went off in the bus. I was in no hurry to get away and stayed on for an hour talking to the students.

I set off for Delhi and drove up into Mehrauli just as the farmers were coming in from the fields. Dust, that fine cement-colored Indian dust, hung folded around the tombs; black and white goats trod the narrow paths on their delicate, high-hoofed feet. By the Mehrauli tank the dhobis were gathering up their washing, and squirrels with striped backs bounded along the broken walls.

I drove slowly, dodging the cattle on the roads and watching the scene slide past—the splendid archaic figures of women bending over the wells, the sad-faced oxen, the peacocks on the tombs. And I felt it drag and tear away like plaster from a wound. I was not consciously happy up there amongst the tanks and tombs of the old cities, but I still felt master of my own life. Work exerted its mechanical disciplines, although decisions I believed I was making were in fact made for me by remote forces that I took for granted and had long ago learned to obey. Ahead of me was that part of the day I could no longer control, and another evening with nothing to do that seemed any better than anything else.

I knew a lot of people in Delhi, but they seemed hazy at that time and without any striking identity, as though my mental eyesight were failing me and I could no longer distinguish their salient features. With Indians I was impatient, with Europeans bored. I had nothing to contribute, and nothing that was said bit into my mind. The only person I really wanted to see was Shankar, but though I knew he had returned from Calcutta this seemed impossible. Sometimes in the evenings when I walked round Connaught Circus I hoped I might run into him. To meet like that, to be jolted by surprise into an impulse of affection, seemed the only way to bridge a gulf that was now immense, because it had started by being imperceptible.

But most of my evenings were spent in my hotel room, reading, and writing to Pamela.

Letters were coming from her twice a week now. The sort of letters that I found easy to answer.

One night I wrote to her:

No one likes to be told again and again that in the most important relationship of his life he has failed. Failed in love, failed in understanding, failed in duty. . . . You keep saying that the first years of our marriage were full of affection and happiness. They were too, but they are gone, and we're older now. If it's the loss of that early happiness that distresses you then you're fighting futilely against the inevitable. If you want me to love you as an inexperienced young man in his twenties loved a virgin hardly out of her teens, you're asking the impossible. Can't you accept the fact of our maturity? A relationship doesn't have to lose quality just because it changes. It needn't be worse. It's simply different.

It was a pompous, sententious letter, full of lies. For I could see no quality in the relationship I had with her now. I seemed to have no feeling for her at all. Her miseries reminded me of

Fred and his cold. Why must her sufferings, the loss of youth, the loss of love, be so much worse than anyone else's? Why must she wail on and on, when others swallowed their medicine and smiled?

I wrote to her without hope or intention of soothing her fears. I wrote out of boredom. And habit. And perhaps too because pain, another's pain, helped me to overcome the sense of dreary inertia that was pressing on my life. Somewhere, far away, a nerve was throbbing.

On Christmas Day I received a telegram, which simply said, "I love you, Pamela."

Christmas Day. And first came Alisulman, with his marigold garland and his greedy eyes. Then the dhobi, suddenly arriving with two weeks' back washing and all the buttons sewn on. Nur, the sweeper—but how could you feel uncharitable to that stick-like figure crouching too close to the ground for effective importunity? The postman. Another postman. And, an hour later, yet another. And just when I had slammed my door on all postmen, there came yet another—whose face was familiar, who indeed might have been the authentic one—and the fear of inflicting injustice that makes a victim out of every European in India extracted another ten rupees from my pocket. Barbers, tailors, cooks. . . . Last of all a small, beautiful boy, who claimed to be the dhobi's son and responsible for handkerchiefs. Shreds of torn rag, illusive, vagrant cotton squares. . . . I now had few of my own, but possessed several entitled E. Szekeley and one of delicate make, called Sylvia.

With our stringy chicken dinner we were supplied with paper caps and crackers that had got damp and wouldn't go off. In the evening I was asked by Sir Malcolm to that most dismal of all Indian functions—a Christmas party where English and Americans tried to forget that they were homesick for holly and robins in the snow. The turkey was probably a peacock, one of those vaguely sacred birds that you mustn't kill. I stayed late, not because I was enjoying myself but to delay going back to the hotel.

The New Year was coming up, and then at least I could get away from Delhi.

Chapter Twelve

THE PLANE WAS SAID TO BE LEAVING AT DAWN. THE CHAUKIDAR still slept on his charpoy by the gate as I left the hotel, and no sweepers were yet about. Yesterday's rubbish still littered the face of India, and yesterday's footprints still showed in her dust. The roads looked enormously wide and above them the trees hung motionless, without a bird stirring.

At the airport a long wait, for to guard against traditional Indian lateness you were asked to put in an appearance much earlier than was necessary. And the plane was delayed. Miserable, shivering peons with thin, unshaven faces and the big, beautiful, stupid eyes of the underfed stationed themselves before the only radiator, and bearers, their heads wrapped up like suet puddings, carried here and there a small case.

When I walked out onto the runway the sun was putting out its first rays—too pale to print a shadow. The wings of the waiting plane glittered softly, and the dome of Safdar Jang's tomb, rising up behind a long crenelated wall, glowed rosy pink, like the bud of a peony.

The small plane carried four officials, and that inevitable family, looking defenseless and displaced, that you encounter even on the big international flights. A popeyed young man with bones like a grasshopper; a shy wife with huge kohled eyes and a stud in her nose; a baby with a frilled bonnet and three young children wearing clothes many sizes too large and not looking like children at all, but like small, crumpled-up adults—already subdued by life and wise to sorrow. They filled the plane with innumerable baskets and bundles; they seemed to be carrying with them all they possessed; they sat still, mute, with a look of ineffable sadness in their eyes.

We flew low over diplomatic enclave and out toward Sultan Gori's tomb. The land beneath looked barren and brown, the dry watercourses showing like jagged wounds with unsealed lips. Occasional hills stuck up from the plane like blunted thorns, but did not interrupt it; on and on it rolled to the rim of the sky, where a glowing haze suggested infinity.

I had brought books with me but did not open them. I kept looking down on the old worn-out face of India, over whose brown monotonies we trailed our tiny shadow. It refreshed me. Immensity is always refreshing. And suffering—other people's suffering—always chastening. A bitter conviction had lodged in my mind—a belief that I had lived my life deprived of its finest and commonest gift. But now for the first time in weeks I shook myself loose from the grip of self-pity.

The airstrip had been cleared from miles of surrounding jungle. A group of officials waited by a jeep. A Hindu god, called

Sacksena, shook my hand—one of the original hierarchy, Indra perhaps, or Vishnu, in the old solemn days before Krishna dallied with milkmaids at Vrindaban. He was District Education Officer and his assistant, Koli, put marigold garlands around my neck. Koli was neat and oiled, with a quantity of big, white teeth, forever on show. Smiling, but not talking, and always stepping back and getting out of the way. The sort of man you went on not noticing for days until you realized that he was the origin of everything that happened around.

We drove to the Circuit House—a relic of the British Raj— stately, pillared, white, overlooking a lake. Two peepul trees grew in the compound, and from these, from morning till night, bee eaters flashed out and dipped in the air, like myriads of emerald butterflies. Prasad, with a retinue of officials, held court on the veranda.

We looked at the site for the new College—some abandoned buildings infested with birds that had built their nests inside its empty rooms and splashed white droppings over its floors.

An itinerary appeared from Koli's shirt pocket. I looked over it, like royalty, and saw myself used to the last of my strength on operations that would have been better served by a trained nurse, a film star, a WHO health inspector, a kindergarten assistant, the matron of a hospital and a manufacturer of razor blades. Protests were fruitless and disregarded. People had come from far and wide . . . all had been arranged. Perhaps royalty fares no better.

A V.I.P., no matter how humble, must see things. This is a necessity, not for him but for the things he sees. The fact of his presence confers a blessing; virtue moves out of him and informs whatever he is being shown—the canal, the model village, the domestic science school. The fact of his visiting these places is sometimes the only solid proof of their existence, and many a half-dead project stirs sluggishly and shakes off its dust to confront him. Such was my function. A talisman, an effigy carried over the heads of the crowd. A presence that proved the concern of the world.

Picnics began to intrude. We turned aside to look at temples and waterfalls—also, it would seem, needing assurance, proof. Our party swelled. One jeep became two and then three. Some of the hospital staff joined us. A journalist, hearing about us in Benares from Prasad—who had now left and was seeking relatives in that holy city—got on the first available train and was in time for the final week.

Friendships formed on the instant and blossomed over food and tireless talk. They were all coming to England. They would visit me. I would visit them. We would write one another letters. They might get scholarships, mightn't they? Well, if not UNESCO, perhaps British Council? Perhaps. . . .

Then, all of a sudden Sacksena got bored, and a school and a local papermaking industry abruptly disappeared from the itinerary. The journalist, who, having joined the retinue rather late, was still enthusiastic, tried to make something out of a piece of headless sculpture in a cave, but Sacksena had remembered that he must return two of the jeeps to the hospital, so that the piece of sculpture, which on Tuesday had been one of the wonders of India, turned out on Wednesday to be so insignificant that there was some doubt as to its being there at all.

Koli said it was time we were moving on.

"Where?" I asked.

He mentioned a small state adjacent to our present frontiers.

We left quietly, just the two of us; the others had exhausted their good will and only the journalist and the doctor turned up to say goodbye.

I hadn't liked Koli when I first met him. He was very vain. He always carried a comb in his shirt pocket and frequently took this out and pulled it through his thick, oiled hair. If we went into a room with a mirror in it, he would sit directly before it and address his words into his own unflagging smile, as though with so much beauty before him it was impossible to look elsewhere. But he was friendly and efficient and by now I had grown quite fond of him. I said, "Koli, would it be possible to take this part of the trip a little more easily?"

"I too am tired," he generously admitted, and drove on an atrocious road fifty miles off our route to show me a temple—he knew I was interested in temples—which, when we got there, turned out to be a waterfall. Koli liked waterfalls.

We reached our destination in the late afternoon. It was one of a thousand Indian towns, concentrated into a dense, crowded center with a few old buildings—the palace, the bazaars—and slowly thinning out through wide dusty roads to its straggling perimeter.

I was tired—the waterfall episode had annoyed me—but Koli was in high spirits. He was very excited about the resthouse we would be staying in. He kept telling me how much I would like it.

I walked around the big circular hall, and he watched me out of the corner of his eye, trying to disguise his eagerness and pride.

I said, "Now, why do you like this place better than our old Circuit House?"

He was a careful young man and took his time thinking up a reply. "There is more Art here."

"Too much."

He had found a mirror—there were many—and, looking into it but forgetting to smile, repeated "Too much?" He did not feel there could ever be too much.

The Maharajah, he told me, the grandfather of the present ruler, who had assembled all this magnificence, was now a very old man. A hundred and twenty years old. Later, the khansama told me he was ninety-nine. Death, in any case, stared him in the face and had already laid its chilly hand on his old dominion. Dust sheets covered the broken brocaded chairs and a grubby canvas had been spread on the floor to preserve what remained of the carpet. Blue watered silk hung down in strips from the walls; in the hideous contorted mirrors our reflections showed gray and indistinct, like ghosts.

We walked about, dodging tables, chairs and snarling toothy heads raised up from skins on the floor.

Koli, sensing that I was not giving the full flush of my appreciation to this showpiece of the state, began to dispense information. "Chandelier. . . ." He pointed to clusters of dangling glass bound together by cobwebs, which themselves were shadowy with dust. "It is the largest in the world."

"It isn't, you know."

"It isn't?" He had been doubtful all along and acquiesced.

"Mirrors . . . vases . . . it is all Art. This is Hindu god." Krishna, chubby as the child in Millais's "Bubbles," and as blue as a hyacinth.

"The Maharajah." As a young boy, as a man in a coat of cloth of gold, on horseback, on an elephant, in a striped blazer captaining a cricket team, in upstanding white whiskers as a grand old man.

"Tiger," declared Koli, stretching out a declamatory hand.

Two, severely stuffed, sat on either side of the door, their tails curled about them and fangs forever bared. Splendid barbaric skins hung stretched upon the walls, and flat-topped predatory heads snarled out of wooden shields. They filled the room with cruelty and menace. The air was thick with the smell of their mothy fur.

Koli came to another mirror, a vile affair of glass branches, leaves and flowers. Pulling out his comb, he began to smooth his hair. "All this is Art."

"The tigers?" I asked.

"Not the tigers. They are animals."

I could not stand such homage paid to so many unworthy objects. "I'll tell you what Art is. It is the sculptures we saw last week at Khajuraho."

"That is not Art," said Koli. "That is religion."

His contention was irrefutable and, humbled, I said no more. It had occurred to me that perhaps all around me indeed *was* Art—if Koli thought so. And as so often happens in India, I felt one of my healthiest convictions—strong, long maintained and long unexamined—grow weak and falter.

The sculptures in question—liquid with movement, sensual and passionate, yet tender and serene—had not appealed to Koli and, suspecting me of lasciviousness, he disapproved of my admiring them. For a Hindu, he was a bit of a prude. Picking hairs out of his comb, he shook them to the floor and spoke severely. "They are pornographic. Do you know the reason for this pornographic sculpture?"

I wondered what theory would come out now. I had already heard half a dozen, all of inspired silliness. "It is a test. If you can walk three times around the temple looking at the figures in those positions and can still keep your mind fixed upon God, then you are a good man. Let us look at the bedroom."

We went out to a veranda enclosed in ornamental cast-iron railings that had been painted pea green and set with panels of stained glass. Here life still throbbed sluggishly. A bundle of rags, erupting at one end into stiff clotted locks of white hair, stirred on a charpoy. Cooking pots and broken sandals littered the floor. And the khansama, who alone had charge of all this decaying magnificence, squatted over a charcoal fire, fanning the flames under a blackened kettle without handle or spout. He wore a frayed red coat that had probably been his uniform when the state was still princely. He had not shaved for days or washed his clothes perhaps for months. He stank. But he had been a member of the Maharajah's retinue and, standing up, he saluted us as we went past. The stained sunlight, piercing the windows, crossed his body in sashes of bronze and blue.

The bedroom was a queer shape; the outer wall, leading to a balcony, long and convex; the inner, leading to the room we had just left, short and concave; and the two side walls slanting at angles. It looked as if it might once have been an accepted shape—square or oblong—and had been sharply tugged at the corners and kicked in the middle. It was arched, pillared, molded and carved. Red and blue glass inlay glittered on the walls. Filthy mattresses made for larger beds slopped down to the floor, and mosquito nets hung in rags from iron rods.

The khansama in his red coat stood stiffly by the door. "Are you English, sahib?"

"Yes," I said, and turned my back on him. His broken yellow teeth and squinting eyes repelled me. The present Maharajah, out of his diminished resources, still went on paying him for doing nothing.

I felt a sudden acute distress. "Koli, this place is a piece of history now. It should either be kept as a museum or, if you don't like looking at that bit of history, pull it down!"

But in India nothing is pulled down and nothing is cleared away. Palaces decay, but they are not demolished.

We sat down, one on either side of a marble-topped table. Koli dragged a finger across it and said, "It is dirty. I shall tell the khansama to send for a sweeper. Why should the Maharajah care? All this is over now. Government has its own Circuit House on the other side of the river."

"You mean there's *another* Circuit House?"

"Of course. This is not Government."

"Then why are we here?" He looked baffled. There was more Art here. "Never mind. It's interesting. I shall never forget it." Dully the glass walls glittered. A door sprang open as a breath of wind stirred the trees outside. Cobwebs and mosquito nets lifted and swayed. "Put the plaque of the Archeological Society on it," I said. "Or burn it down and throw that old villain on the funeral pyre."

"He is an old man," said Koli softly. "The Maharajah keeps him on, but think of the servants they had in the old days. Perhaps fifty in this place, perhaps a hundred. How can they pay such servants now? And how can he live?"

His tenderness shamed me, and I thought how ruthless we

Westerners are, with our logical antiseptic revolutions. Old men may choose to live in the rubbish heap and finish their days amongst the ghosts of their youth. But not in our forthright and sensible society. Rats might breed, and the smell of the past offends us. I would have lifted the old khansama out of his life and put him to some useful work—and to the long, nagging suffering of displacement.

After I had spent a night in that room I became quite fond of it. In the murky yellow electric light the walls glittered with vulgar merriment and, little knowing how much I should bless the protest of my rebellious body, I got hold of a clean mattress. Not only clean but brand new—straight from the dusty, luminous street of the cotton beaters.

It arrived on my second day, lumped in by the old khansama in the morning; and behold, it fitted the bed. I was trying it out at about three-thirty, having been left in peace by Koli, who was off somewhere visiting friends.

I must have slept, but only for an instant, for when I awoke the quality of light in the room had not changed. But as always, when I came to it from somewhere else—from another room, from outside, from sleep—it startled me. How could anyone have thought it up? Have invented and produced so much shoddy richness, such twisting pillars and arched recesses, brackets, pediments, flowers and leaves, fruits and birds. And yet missed beauty. Not even found beauty by accident. I lay listening with half my mind to the voice that had awakened me.

Then listened with all my mind and thought that I had been tricked. By my own weariness, and by this room that had gone on existing for twenty years, outside life, mirroring day by day in its glassy walls its own unresolved confusions. But the voice went on.

I got up and went out onto the veranda, stepping through pools of red and blue light and into the main hall. Helen sat on the arm of a chair talking to the khansama.

I stood between the tigers at the door and an illusion of movement in their striped skins made me turn with a start of apprehension. She glanced back over her shoulder, showing me her face for an instant, in a look that was too swift to have any meaning. "Have you seen this wonderful roof?" She lifted her head and addressed her words to the faded silk. "Turn it on again, will you?"

The khansama, beaming with happiness, went to the wall and turned a switch. There was a flicker while the electricity seemed to make up its mind whether it would work or not. Then out shone stars and a moon through slits cut in the faded heaven.

"Just look at that. And did you know that he's been to St. Moritz?"

"St. Moritz very good place."

"For the winter sports. With the old Maharajah. And Brighton. Which did you like the best out of all the places you've been to?"

He replied instantly. "I like Clacton best. I like St. Moritz too. St. Moritz very good place."

I crossed the canvas sheet and the tiger skins. I stood close by her chair and saw her shoulders lift a little, and stiffen.

There was nothing more I needed to know. A lot that I didn't—when she had come, how she had found me—but none of it mattered. Her presence was an open capitulation, and at first I felt a flush of greedy conceit. Well, it had taken a long time, and I wasn't so inept after all.

Then, afterward, came that same sense of gravity. Odd, incongruous, considering us both; neither of us what you would call serious people, but normal, healthy, out for a good time and not addicted to suffering. Rather disliking pain. But, looking at her, I seemed to see myself, and I knew that, though miles apart, we had been leading, for the past weeks, identical lives. Long vacant days and sleepless nights had filled her up with voluptuous thoughts and accumulated longings. Then the whole of life adhered to what might be; and what was, dropped its worth. Everything lost, so no costs to count. A human being at large, without possessions. We don't often achieve this felicitous condition, and when she returned my look there was a new reckless courage in her eyes.

I said to the khansama, "That'll do. You can turn it off."

He turned the switch and the stars went out. "There were thirty people in the court when they went to St. Moritz," Helen said. "Did you take elephants?" She was keeping him on purpose, while she settled down and got used to her happiness.

He giggled. "No elephants, Memsahib. Can't take elephants to St. Moritz."

"Hannibal took them over the Alps." And then, for me, she said, "Was the past better?"

"No! You can go now."

He went, and I waited as his big bulk in the doorway shut down the light. I glanced at the door, and in the fragmented, colored light of the veranda I saw him pick up his black, broken kettle and walk to the stairs, and then I put my hands on her shoulders and crushed her against me.

At first it was strange, because I had known her so long in my imagination and had explored every inch of her body in my thoughts. And now this unfamiliar flesh that held my skin and mouth with a moist, magnetic drag. And her lips that were at first muscular, and then soft.

In the end there was still a lot to find out, which is as it should be. I had lived for so long on the surface of her personality, how could I know in an hour what lay beneath that purring golden skin? Chilly, narcissistic vanity or bountiful tenderness? The mosquito nets, hanging down in dusty rags, trailed their shadows over a body in metamorphosis, still mysterious and equivocal, as yet not fully claimed, either by disappointment or delight. Her old identity shed, yet not remade. Not yet quite turned and curved into that female segment which was the other half of our astounding love.

Once she said to me, "Something has happened. . . ."

The sun was low and a long yellow bolt, spinning with dust, impaled the floor, like the sign of a deity's attention. Then she turned on her side, shifting the colored web that clothed her skin; a shivering dapple of crimson, purple and blue. A wind had sprung up, tossing a tree and flashing its shadows about, so that all around us the walls giggled and winked. And I thought that all the confusions in the room—the bitter tournaments of East and West, the misunderstandings, the uncertainties, the pitiful aspirations and divided loves—were spinning about us as though upon their point of resolution. We might have been lying in the dark of a neurotic mind that is suddenly pierced by a simple shining thought.

"I have something to tell you. . . ."

But I felt only the dimmest curiosity. What had happened was in the past, and for what had happened now to have happened at all, the future must have taken a new turn. I don't even remember whether she herself told me or whether I heard it for the first time from Fred. Later that night, drinking beer on the resthouse veranda—the Government resthouse on the other side of the river.

He had been out all day, tiger shooting with the Maharajah. No tigers, but the Maharajah had given him a crate of beer as a consolation prize. So there he was, dispensing hospitality to me, to Koli and to his own little retinue of Indian officials. Helen, he let me know in an undertone, had not liked the Maharajah. Occasionally she got a down on someone. Just like that. Which was why she had preferred to stay and look at the town. Which was why she had found me. And what luck that she had! For there we might have sat, each on his own side of the river in our little guesthouse, and never met.

He had had a marvelous day, full to the brim with princely extravagance. In the gardens cars drove you from the swimming pool to the tennis courts, and to a marble pavilion on an island in the lake you went in a motorboat. There were white peacocks on the lawn and the Ranee was charming. When he was in the States he was going to buy her an electric egg beater.

"In the States?"

"Elly, you haven't told him?" Well, good! For now he had the delight of telling me himself. He was going to New York in February, on a conference. A big affair with delegates from all countries—a further attempt to co-ordinate international geophysical research. Fred was to present the picture for northern India. It seemed extraordinary that he should have any picture to impart, but perhaps he was adept in inventing one. It would all take a fortnight, but you could always count on Fred to make a greedy snatch after more time. Not leave—not on your life—that would be owed to him. He had managed to persuade Sir Malcolm—and, incidentally, Paris—to give him a further week in New York for talks about equipment that was wanted for the new program, and a return trip through Paris with a further three days there to discuss his "problems." He had worked it all out carefully so that the third day of his Paris assignment fell on a Friday, and he could then legitimately take the weekend off. Totaled up, his time abroad would exceed a month.

"Is Helen going too?"

"We can't afford the trip for her," said Fred. "It would take all the profits."

"Profits?"

The Mercedes was to be sold. Ruplal had already got hold of a buyer, and the application to sell was on its way through the Ministry. When he was in the States he would buy a Cadillac.

Halfway through his story Helen slipped away inside and I had the feeling that suddenly she felt ashamed. Of Fred? Of herself? Of me? Of our threefold exploitation of one another? My less open and well-proportioned spirit suffered no qualms.

"Listen, Elly. . . ."

"Yes." She came to the door and stood looking out at us.

"You'll never guess! He's got a silver bath."

"Did you bathe in it?"

"You are joking. Elly always likes a joke. Of course not, but he showed it to me. He's very proud of it. Only it's rather dirty. You wouldn't have known it was silver at all."

He left three weeks later. February the fourteenth. A cold, sunny, spicy morning. We took him to the airport, Helen and I. We saw him smile and wave through the doors of the Departure Lounge. And then we turned and walked together back to my car. Both of us quiet. Both of us holding our happiness back—even now afraid to believe in it.

Everything looked perfect, almost too perfect. The day before, Giles had rung up to say he would be away for two weeks and did I want his flat.

As we drove back into town, for the first time that winter there was dust in the air, and the trees had suddenly broken into fresh leaf. Old leaves had been swept up into little piles, each putting out its thread of blue smoke that drifted into the gardens and hung in a pearly vapor over the lawns. So our love affair began in the first spring weather—that Indian spring which is the shortest in the world; one week, perhaps two, then swiftly spoils into summer.

Chapter Thirteen

HER CABLE, GRITTY WITH DUST AND MARKED WITH THE RING OF a wet glass, lay for three days on Agawalla's desk. She might have expected as much. She had her view of India, where intentions are forever frustrated, actions forever incomplete, and where nobody bothers to pass on messages—at least not to the person for whom they were intended.

I told her what had happened, and Agawalla, who had a scapegoat in Alisulman, was prepared to support me. But later she began to believe that I had bribed him to suppress the cable. Pamela regarded the past as most people look on the future, not as a place where events have unalterably happened but as an area in time where anything may yet take place.

Her plane got in at 1 A.M. Most planes coming to New Delhi seem to prefer the early morning hours, which are appropriately empty for the dropping of yet more life into that bursting peninsula. An eerie and discomforting time, for India is its people, and India's beauty is movement and color. With life dispersed from her chaotic roads, there is little left but ugliness and the harsh face of her poverty.

Later I had to live through this night as Pamela experienced it. She gave me not only its broad events but such meticulous elaborations as a twist of hair in a wastepaper basket—all reproduced in the glare of a memory that enjoyed a loving addiction to fear and pain.

Expecting me to be there, she had looked for the shape of my body in the thin crowd that slouched over the enclosure railings. She waved. The headlights of a fuel lorry turned and glared in her face.

In February, the Punjab night has a chill invigorating edge. Indians, who feel the cold like pain, wore shawls around their shoulders and folded scarves across their mouths. She felt oddly disappointed, having remembered the heat and irrationally expected it, for she had come fortified with resolutions and ready for hardships that were perversely withheld.

In the Transit Lounge she waited with the other passengers for the Health Officer to be ready to pass them through. He was in no hurry, and talked with another official—probably a friend. The electric lights had no shades; crushed-out cigarettes in unemptied ashtrays gave off a stale, bitter smell. When her turn came, her health certificate was not in her passport where she had put it.

"You must have health certificate," said the Health Officer, looking up at her with staring, unkind eyes. But it wasn't in her handbag, her overnight bag or the pockets of her coat. She went through the passport again, page by page, and found it between two pages that had stuck together—a tube of ointment for her dermatitis having lost its cap. He could find nothing wrong with it, although, smelling out an opportunity to bully, he looked hard and long.

There was nothing wrong with her passport either, but the incident with her health certificate had shaken her nerves. In the Customs she waited for her luggage to arrive and filled in a currency form. The official here, responding to her blond, flickering prettiness, was talkative and intimately friendly. India, as always, was either too far away or too close.

She said, "My husband is meeting me. I expect he's in the foyer."

"He will come, Madam. He will come." Yes, yes. He flicked his fingers and wagged his head from side to side in a way which she remembered. It had always irritated her, and it irritated her now, but she was grateful to him for his friendliness. She could not see into the foyer, for the door was crammed with Indians who had come to meet their friends. But she thought that I might have stood behind and waved at her.

There were only three bearers to carry the luggage in—all of them, it would seem, chosen for their physical frailty. Beautiful, stupid eyes; thin, sparrow-like bodies, lost in enormous clothes. They had no carts or trolleys; they brought the luggage by hand, one case at a time. In between trips they stood about engaged in arguments that totally absorbed them, so that they seemed to forget why they were there. A dozen small cases stood in a row on the Customs bench. The porters waited, staring and dreaming.

"I have a big brown case," said Pamela urgently. She turned to the Customs official. "None of my luggage is here."

"What is your name, Madam?"

"Mrs. Mardellis."

"Are you in transit, Madam?"

"No, I am stopping off here."

"How long are you staying and what is the name of your hotel?"

She could see the interrogation heading off into some totally irrelevant topic and began to get angry. "What does it *matter?* My luggage isn't here."

Two Italian girls said that their luggage had not arrived either.

"What are we waiting around here for?" said a tall, stooped American carrying an attaché case. "What's holding us up?"

"Look at those men!" cried Pamela, fortified by the general complaints. Their dull eyes turned to regard her and she remembered that she hated them, for their poverty and stupidity, and for their unwillingness to do anything about it. Creatures without dignity and courage, who would neither serve nor contend, but tunneled at the foundations of life, like worms.

"Madam," said the Customs official, "luggage will come."

Slightly larger cases began to arrive. Pamela's big case was one of the last.

Outside an engine started and loudly roared. Was it the bus leaving? She was shaken by an attack of panic, as though this were the last bus that would ever leave that place—that no-place-on-earth, with its naked electric globes and its look of not being anywhere at all.

"Madam, bus will wait."

At the door leading to the foyer she knew a moment of vivid happiness when her whole future life was displayed before her as charming and simple as a young girl's vision of love. There I was, coming toward her. "Darling . . . I can't tell you how sorry I am. The car broke down. . . . Darling. . . ."

But I was not there, and though hope had seized her for only a split second, without it she was thrown into brutal despair.

In the bus they sat waiting for half an hour and all her useless fears wasted around her. Passengers were asking one another whether they had reservations. Some who had had found it difficult getting them. It was the middle of the tourist season and the big hotels were full.

At two-thirty the bus began to move. They rattled and shook through a darkness edged by bushes, huts and telegraph wires. And Pamela, looking out through the window, realized India as one can never realize it anywhere else. The irredeemable people, the debased towns, the raped land.

The road curved, encircled a roundabout. Radical roads pointed in different directions. Now she remembered that such roads promised a destination—a city, a garden, a tomb—and found each an identical and featureless degradation. Again the bushes, the huts, the telegraph wires. A cow, bony in its bag of skin with the long dewlap hanging in leathery folds; a stained wall, streaked with a broad red splash, like a spurt of blood. By a little smoldering fire a hooded figure rocked back and forth, chanting in mysterious distress. Suddenly Delhi began to sprout up around them. Row upon row of flat, boxy houses, silent and white, standing side by side on the naked beaten ground.

They stopped at the Ashoka first, putting off passengers who had booked, but there were only two vacancies for those who hadn't. So the farsighted, the rich and fortunate left the bus; and the indigent, the careless and unlucky remained.

Pamela spoke to the driver. "Will you put me down at the Mayfair?"

"I will, Madam." He had large, gentle eyes and she trusted him.

A German couple had bookings at the Imperial and on the way they stopped at two other hotels but both were full.

Now the wide, tree-lined roads looked clean and affluent. The handsome white houses with their broad verandas and pillared porches stared out over lawns that surrounded them like moats, each house a fortress, guarding its privacy against poverty, disease, despair.

"You could put me down at the Mayfair," Pamela said. "It's not far away."

"Madam, we go to Imperial first. Then we go to that place."

The Italian girls went in to see if they could get a room. Then came out, laughing, to take their luggage from the bus. It had been an adventure. They would gladly have stayed up all night. There was no food, they said excitedly. All the staff were on strike and they wouldn't even get any breakfast.

Only two passengers remained—Pamela and a French journalist with a lined, sardonic face. Fifty yards down the road the bus jerked to a halt. It was three-fifteen. The trees shuffled as sleeping crows croaked and stirred. Human beings lay on the pavement, bound up in rags, like unburied dead.

"This is a marvelous country," said the journalist.

"It's always like this." The only thing to do was to enjoy these ludicrous events, she thought, but there was a sensation of vacancy within her. Exhaustion took hold of her like sickness and it was agony not to lie down. The driver pulled back the front seat and looked for tools. Then, going around to the engine, he began striking it hard, decisive blows with some implement that looked like a piece of lead pipe.

"*Mon Dieu!*" The Frenchman half rose to his feet. A cyclist rode by, ringing his bell at the empty road. He wobbled and slid to the ground. Wheeling his bike across, he stood looking into the open hood of the bus. He made no offer to help, asked nothing. He simply stood, breathing in the sweet stench of another's bad luck.

The driver pulled down the hood and got back in his seat. Suddenly they were moving. "*Mon Dieu!*" said the Frenchman again. "I am going to try the Grand," he told Pamela. "I have been told that it's not too bad and it's cheap."

The Grand was on one of the radial roads off the Circus, and while he went in Pamela said to the driver, "Will you take me now?"

"Where is that, Madam?" He looked at her as though for the first time, and again it was a face she remembered. The eyes direct and dull, the words coming quick and easy. The smooth racial facility in the art of evasion.

Pamela said softly, "The Mayfair Hotel."

"Madam, it is better you stay here."

She felt anger beginning within her. Then breaking loose and charging over her mind. "*I have to go to the Mayfair!*"

"This very good hotel. Mayfair not good. This better."

The hotel looked dark, mean and dirty. A sign hung cockeyed over the door. One of the letters had fallen off. Torn bamboo blinds that no one had bothered to roll up flapped against the stained veranda columns. It was only anger that kept her from crying.

She tried to remember what had happened to induce this rage, this sense of despairing frustration. But nothing had happened, or only something very trivial. And it wasn't strength that India asked of you—it was compassion, and patience, second by second and every second. You grasped at thorns, ready for pain. They turned soft in your hands, left a slime on your skin. "Can't you people even *lie* efficiently?"

The Frenchman came back to pull his case off the rack. "What's it like?" she asked.

He shrugged his shoulders. "God knows. They've got a room for you. I asked them."

"Thank you." She felt his casual kindness fall upon her like an insult. She did not attract him; he liked composed, debonair, *soignée* women.

"It is a good hotel," said the driver softly. She turned on him savagely, but there was nothing to say—no standards mutually held with which to confront him.

The hotel clerk showed her a long narrow room that had once been large but was now divided into two by a thin partition. His manner was respectful and polite, and he seemed to wish that she might be comfortable. But when he had gone and she was alone, she was aware less of her own identity than of countless others—only partially erased. A woman with long hair who had needed big pins to put it up. A man who had picked his teeth. Someone who had used face tissues and thrown them into the wastepaper basket. The carpet was sticky with the prints of vanished feet.

India is deceitful in recollection. She had remembered tall women with towers of shining pots upon their heads, and green parrots hanging like fans on the domes of tombs. There had been kindnesses and sudden moments of beauty. I am older now, she had thought, and wiser. . . . Perhaps I could live there and be happy.

Cockroaches in the bath waved their repulsive tentacles. She edged them down the plughole with her shoe, and then put in the plug to lock them in the drains.

Still wearing her underwear, she crept into the gray, mold-smelling sheets and tried to sleep.

But sleep would not come. The room was light, as though dawn were about to break, and the departing night paraded before her with all its half-completed acts and broken purposes. Nothing large to challenge the better part of the human spirit. All trivial, exacting trivial responses. She had arrived, and no one waited. She had set out for one destination and found another. In the end she had put her fate in the hands of a stranger who seemed to be good—and then was too bored to be kind.

She took, to be on the safe side, two Nembutal, and slept till eleven o'clock the next morning.

Chapter Fourteen

SHE SAT ON MY BED, HER LEGS TUCKED BENEATH HER, AND HER body and face oddly unassembled. She looked like the last survivor of a conflagration, with all life's certainties smoking around her.

Surprisingly, I was prepared for this moment, and found at hand a ready-made set of mechanical responses. I crossed the room. I kissed her. I said that it was nice to see her and what a surprise. As my lips broke from her soft, cold mouth, I noticed—over her head and behind her—a moth, hooked on the window screen like a collector's specimen. Brown wings with a deep-blue eye, like the eye on a peacock's tail.

She must have followed my glance. She was quick to understand me. She had measured my moods for twelve years, and the smallest emotional fluctuations never escaped her.

"Richard! You didn't even hear me!"

"Yes I did," I said, hearing her words then for the first time, as though my mind had taken them in and stored them. "You said it was wonderful to see me."

I pulled up a chair and sat down. A small, round table stood between us. One of those ugly pieces of Indian bedroom furniture—a peculiar bit of hoop-shaped wood held it up, instead of some plain, honest-to-God legs. When does India ever look facts in the face? I felt utterly exhausted, and there was a sensation of soreness in my chest, which I suppose was suffering.

"Why didn't you meet me at the airport?"

"I didn't know you were coming."

"I *cabled* you."

"I didn't get your cable."

"Oh God! This country. . . . Richard, it was *awful!* I can't tell you how awful it was. I thought I would never get out of that place. And the hotel . . ."

She leaned toward me, her body tipped over the bed and holding up her face as though to make sure I got the full dose of her distress. I was supposed to take her in my arms and say I was sorry. I saw the scene. I took it in. I could not move.

Her very first words revived the old story over again. I had failed her. . . . She had signaled me and I had not responded. Resentment and anger began to work within me.

Then Alisulman brought tea. So we had time to pull out from that little mess and start again.

She kept saying, "You can't believe what it was like! You can't believe. . . ."

She clenched her fists and struck them up and down on her knees. The violence of her movements brought the hair tumbling over her face, and she shook it back in a gesture that had long ago hardened into a nervous mannerism. Pamela's hair was her one radiant feature, a thick, nutty gold, framing a face like a flower—pretty and boneless, beginning to smudge and crumple. I looked at the spongy, wavering lines of her cheek, at her frilly lips, and thought that I liked a face that was built perceptibly upon the skull, with the flesh close to the contours of the bone.

I said, "Why didn't you write? We both agreed that it was better for you to stay in London. When you make an agreement with someone, you usually consult them before you break it. You should at least have let me know."

"You mean you would have said I couldn't come. . . ."

"I don't know what I would have said. You haven't given me the chance to say anything, have you? It's not the first time this sort of thing has happened. If you blunder into situations which you know are going to cause you distress, you can't blame other people for letting you down. Unless of course that's your object all along."

"What do you *mean*? Why should I want to blame you? Oh, darling, if only I didn't sometimes. Perhaps I do ask too much of you."

"Too much! My God! How was I meant to know that at one-thirty last night my wife would arrive in Delhi and expect me to be at the airport to meet her. Some little voice whispering away inside?"

She was weeping into her hands. "Whenever I most need you, you're not there. I'll never forget how you walked out that day and left me to get rid of those cats. Thirty-eight! Thirty-eight! I'll never forget that day as long as I live!"

I watched her cry. I felt exhausted with misery. When I spoke I kept my voice gentle.

"Six months ago you and I agreed that it was better for you to stay in London. My work is in India. You don't like India. You don't even like other people liking it. Liking India to you is the sign of some sort of depravity."

"Not depravity. Hardness, indifference to all that suffering. . . . It's the hypocrisy . . . taking all that money. . . ."

"Pamela, I can live in this country and like it and be quite comfortable. I don't happen to share your liberal indignation. In my mind it is sentimental, wrongheaded and as often as not an expression of your own deficiencies. Dirt, poverty and sickness exist here, but not as you see them. They don't have the meanings you attribute to them. Things that horrify you because you think they are important are insignificant here, and the important things, for Indians, you don't even notice. If you had real understanding you'd stop feeling outraged and wanting to change them."

"And I suppose you're understanding all the time."

"Of course I'm not. I think it's very difficult for any Westerner to understand—to look over the top of what repels him. But this country shows us our differences. It always does. You have to face issues here; they are pushed under your nose like a leper's sores. And you and I are divided on every point. I accept things, you're an improver. You're a child of this century, and perhaps I'm not. You fight all the circumstances around you. You even fight yourself and me. All I want to do is live my life and enjoy it. It may sound like a mean ambition but if you want to make a moral issue of it, I regard this as my duty."

"And you don't regard it as your duty, I suppose, to attack some of the social evils."

"What social evils?"

"Oh my God!"

"I suppose you're talking about caste. People usually do."

"Well, all right. Caste. . . . You can't pretend that it's a particularly pretty business."

"Listen, Pamela. Caste is very old. I haven't read the literature that explains its origins. I don't even begin to understand its implications, neither have I thought of the consequences of abolishing it, even supposing one could, but I am not here to interfere with the way in which other people wish to live or to pass judgments on customs I don't understand."

She fell silent and I saw her brows knit as she looked back upon an opportunity for pain that had passed her unexploited.

"So we're divided on every point. You're saying that I shouldn't have come."

"I think we are both happier away from each other."

She lay on her face. Attacks of crying shook her body. Then she would lie utterly still, as if she had lost consciousness.

What tenacity, I thought, what unscrupulous strength! But she had got me now. I sat beside her, engrossed in my guilt, in my reluctant but inescapable compassion. I put my arms about her and pulled her up so that she lay limply against me.

"Pamela, why come all the way to India just to tell me that I hate you?"

"Darling! Darling! I know you don't! I know you love me. God! Why am I such a fool? I need you, darling, to remind me what a fool I am."

Her words were like the responses to a prayer. So familiar that only by an effort of concentration could I understand them.

I talked to her gently. Comforting words for the poor little girl were asked for now. "Go and have a shower and put on a clean dress. Then I'll take you for a drive round Delhi. We'll have dinner in town. You'll feel better then. Just pull yourself together like a good girl and we'll talk later."

While she was changing I went to tell Agawalla to put another bed in the room. Outside the clouds were pink and the cattle egret were coming over in their snowy battalions. Soni's granddaughters played badminton, hitting the shuttlecocks high in the air, their long dopattas streaming behind them.

I walked over to the new annex and knocked on Helen's door. But she was not there and I remembered that she had gone to a late afternoon concert—one of New Delhi's pitiful little charities for the alleviation of India's immense distress.

I wrote her a brief note and slipped it under the door. It stated the facts. That was all. Anyone could have read it and imagined nothing more than a canceled engagement for dinner.

We got home at ten. We talked till twelve. She told me all she had seen and felt and learned since that day, last September. How she had watched me onto the airport bus and walked away, thinking to herself that she must learn to live without me. And had tried. And could not.

At twelve we went to bed and talked till two. Because I felt sorry for her and could not bear her pain in feeling unwanted, I began to caress her. She kissed me and cuddled against me until I slipped my hand between her legs. Then she snapped them together like a pair of scissors.

"Darling, I'm so sorry! I feel so upset. You don't know what the past three days have been like. I feel . . . I'm so tense. . . . Tomorrow. . . ."

Oh God! As if I minded. . . . But I hated her for rejecting

my tepid, dutiful passion. I could see the future before us like a caricature of the past—each feature more emphatic as time went by.

I said, "Pamela, I am quite prepared to look after you, provide for you and defend you from the molestations of other men. But I can't make you happy. I simply don't know how to go about it. So don't expect it of me."

I got back into my own bed and lay there, my body aching with resentment and longing for its lost delights. The darkness was thick with the smoke of my cigarettes. At about four o'clock she stopped crying and went to sleep.

She was still asleep at seven and when Alisulman knocked with the tea I opened the door quietly and sent him away. I dressed and went over to the new annex. The air had a touch of frost and the morning still hung in haze under the canopies of trees and slanted on the veranda, where Nur shuffled along pushing his rag. Soni, in his pajamas, stood on the balcony, surveying his realm and thinking of God and money.

It was early for me to be visiting Helen; but now I didn't care who saw me or what they thought.

I felt desperate and irresponsible. My mind veered between an exultant despair and the suddenly possible, imminent hope of abandoning Pamela.

Helen, already dressed, was putting something into a suitcase on the bed. I knelt on the floor and, wrapping my arms around her, pressed my head into her belly, into that soft pocket of flesh just above the pelvic bone. I felt her stiffen; then she put her hands on my head and pushed her fingertips through my hair. But her voice was dry, matter-of-fact. "Never mind, Dick. It can't be helped. It would have happened in a week or two anyway."

Already she had retracted her private endearments and handed me back my public name.

I stood up and began kissing her, roughly, searchingly. I crushed and mouthed and soaked her in, as though she might prove efficacious and powerful and so taken into me that no one and nothing could prize us from each other. The most fitting language for this pitiful superstition is love, so I pulled her to the bed. But she hung back, snatching her hands away. "No, Dick! I've got to pack. I'm going away."

She turned away from me, picking up something—a blue blouse that she wore with a white linen skirt. And I saw her walking down a red sanded path, with beds of cannas flaring on either side.

I said, "Helen, don't leave me. I can't live without you." The trite, spoiled words came straight from my heart, as though I were the first ever to speak them.

"Don't be a fool! Anyone can live without anyone else."

But it seemed to me that I was taking for myself not only a woman I loved—happiness, the continuance of my body's pleasure—but the true direction of my nature. There could be other women, further refinements of sensuality, but never again this freedom to be myself, this way of escape from years of misdirection.

She told me that she was going away for the weekend. At the concert she had run into Don and Indra Braden. They were going on a picnic to Agra with Otto and Giles; there was room in Giles' car and Helen must go too. She had declined, but later that evening, after she had read my note and when she hadn't known what to do except that it must be something, she had found herself setting out for the Bradens' house. It was arranged that Giles should pick her up that morning. "He's coming at nine."

I said, "Helen, men and women have been known to divorce and remarry. It's often done. Why do you feel it's impossible for us?"

She said quickly, "*You* do too!"

"I did. I don't now. It's quite ordinary. People are doing it all the time. We could do it too."

"I haven't even thought about it." She spoke carefully, choosing her words with a kind of deliberate caution, as though they might ignite and explode in her face. "I was in love with you . . . all the time . . . just a little bit. And then a lot. And then with Fred going away, I thought . . . it doesn't matter. I didn't know I'd ever feel like this."

Then she let herself go a little, and I held her. And the pulses of our bodies beat together, so that I felt happy, strong and certain of her. We had started our life together as two adventurers. We had fumbled toward each other, pushed by an urgent sensual attraction. Throughout the past two weeks the future had stood over us, but by mutual consent we refused to look at it. We lived from sensation to sensation, and by our neglect of the days ahead, our total concentration upon each other, we had forged ourselves into a formidable unit. Now we seemed less destructible than the obstacles around us.

But I was thinking too fast for Helen and she pushed me away. "Please, Dick . . . you're acting as if everything's settled, and it isn't. I just want some time, and I have to pack. I just want to get away for a day or two."

Chapter Fifteen

JUST TO GET AWAY. . . . IT WAS SOMETHING THAT COULD BE done and therefore seemed like a solution. And in spite of what she had said to me, she was not going away to think but to enjoy herself. Helen did not believe that thought ever accomplished much. Placing more reliance on her senses, she often referred to thought as seeing, and when she asked herself what she now felt about Fred, she did so by evoking his image and looking at it dispassionately, as she might have looked at him had he at that moment walked in through the door. Fondness, touched with contempt—I had taught her that. Before she met me it had never occurred to her to be critical of Fred.

She had finished packing. Seated in front of the mirror, she combed her hair and, looking at her tight, sharp face with the eyes of love, thought she was beautiful. About her in the empty, silent room distress moved like a ghost; but love went on, sweetening her flesh, and it was impossible to feel totally un-happy. Giles knocked on the door and she went to open it with a feeling of gratitude, because whatever one did in one's life, however stupidly and destructively one acted, there remained these familiar unimportant figures, lending stability—uncritical, uncommitted, because they were there by accident and the most they ever felt was curiosity. She wondered if Giles knew how we had used his flat, and felt a kind of love for him. It was a relief to love someone who didn't matter, didn't even know. A casual waste of feeling that made life seem less serious.

His car was outside with Krishan driving.

"Hullo, Mrs. Siegel!" Krishan cried, excited, overfriendly, waving his hand. "We are so glad you changed your mind!" He was in one of his perky, in-love-with-himself moods, and Giles, leaning over, struck him lightly on the cheek. But he smiled and narrowed his eyes, so that Krishan only laughed and, grabbing hold of his wrist, bit his hand.

They drove to the Bradens' house, where Indra, Don and their two children, were making a noisy business of getting ready. The Bradens treated their picnics to correct holiday clothes, and Indra wore blue matador trousers and a green roll-necked sweater. Don looked heavy and square in raw-silk pants and a brown Madras cotton shirt. He was a placid, silent man who had handed the details of his life over to his dynamic wife; but he was not weak, and still made the large decisions.

Babblers pecked at their reflections in the chromium on the headlights, and Otto leaned on the hood as though keeping himself in reserve. He made no attempt to help. The two children dashed back and forth, and his eyes, turning to follow them, showed that he was alive. Bearers pushed baskets into the luggage carrier.

"We'll take one of the children," said Giles when Indra called out, "You are half empty in there."

But the children did not want to be separated, not from their father or from each other.

"I will go with you," said Otto, and unfolded his arms.

"I only want one of the children," said Giles, then added rudely, "Don, you can come."

Helen saw Otto's face become sullen and hard. Giles and Otto had grown to hate each other. Though they went to the same parties, they rarely spoke, and mutual friends stood between them like referees. But they had to be together, so that the other might not be somewhere else.

"I don't mind a child," said Giles, as they set off, "but I'm damned if I'm going to have Otto's great German thighs spread out all over my car. He sweats and when he sweats he smells. They wear those leather things for twenty years without underpants, and you can't wash them, can you? They wear them till their great buttocks spread and then they move into the next size. Think what the inside must be like."

Krishan laughed. "He likes smells, Mrs. Siegel. He tells me I smell of curry. Do you think I smell of curry?"

"Get on with your driving!"

But a moment later Giles was chattering away in his usual vein.

"Now, if I wanted to get out and pee, do you imagine that I could complete that performance, even supposing that it took only thirty seconds. . . ."

"Did you know that the entire population of India could stand side by side on the Isle of Wight. It goes to show that as long as you don't want to sit down, there still is a little room left in the world."

The flat fields slipped by, the road pushing straight ahead like a road in Australia, Helen thought, where the land was also flat but unpeopled and uncluttered. You followed the metaled road and you knew for certain that there, out of sight and a long way away, but directly ahead, was the place to which you were going.

They made it a slow trip, stopping to picnic on the way, and reached Agra in the evening.

They had booked four rooms in the hotel. Indra slept with the children, Don shared with Otto. The rooms were alongside one another, with verandas back and front; they were filled with the big ugly furniture of old Indian hotels. Spaciousness had been won and then filled up; even the high white walls had not been spared. Cords hung down—from lights, from fans, from dirty windows placed high up by the ceiling and left unopened since the departure of the British. Sentimental pictures, strung up on much-mended wire, leaned out as though looking at the floor. Sitting down on the narrow bed, Helen found herself regretting that she had come. But her regret was like sin, and she reprimanded herself for what seemed like a lapse into self-pity.

Next door Krishan laughed and the high, runaway sound was like a warning. She heard Giles' voice. The words were indistinct, but she could read the tone. An ugly, sprawling scene was getting under way.

It offended her, and she went outside to escape it. Helen was rarely angry. The friends she had she kept. She gave what they expected and never expected too much from them. She knew little about the painful, jealous misunderstandings of intimacy, and love for her had been a discovery in depth. In all her married life with Fred she had never raised her voice to him. If he annoyed her, as he sometimes did, she went out or into another room until he was being more pleasant and she found she could like him again.

Lakshmi and Hamilton were playing ping-pong on the veranda at the back of the hotel. Helen took on the boy and defeated him 6–1 with some satisfaction. He had won every game so far and become so cocky he had reduced his sister to tears.

"You're not watching the ball," she told him.

"I was playing much better before." His beautiful mouth drooped and his eyes were limpid with reproach.

"You're not bad." She relented and, throwing the racket down, she wandered into the garden. The exercise had exhilarated her, and she was conscious, as she walked, of her young eager body and the warm air sipping the sweat from her skin.

She passed a bed of cannas, their scarlet flowers like strips of Christmas paper. At a tank beneath a mango tree the mallees were filling their waterskins. Parrots screamed in the thickset leaves and darted out, their flight a long green ribbon thrown down from the trees to the sunflower bed; then back again to perch in the leaves and crack the big brown seeds.

Giles sat on the veranda outside his room.

"Have you seen Krishan?"

"No."

"The rotten little whore."

She wished he had not said it. He seemed to offer her secrets that should have been kept, as though she were one of his own kind who had broken away from the general human pattern of order and decency—an inhabitant of the bad lands where anything might happen. She understood then that Giles knew—

perhaps he had known even before that fortnight in his flat. At any rate he knew now. There were ways . . . servants, spies. He looked at her with his unaffectionate blue gaze and talked as he could never have talked except to someone he had taken into his power.

"It's because he knows he can get away with it," she said at last, when the squalid recital had come to an end. "You've been too generous, and you've given him too much freedom."

"Like my cook cheating me," he said spitefully. "You sound like every memsahib in India."

She shrugged her shoulders. "I've never had to deal with servants. I live in a hotel. But I don't see that it has to be so difficult. I should just be firm and make things clear, and not change my mind."

"They're all parasites," said Giles. "Sponging is all they know, and they're so stupid they can't even be efficient. They really are a most appalling people."

"Why don't you get rid of him?"

"I shall if this goes on," he said without conviction. "That night when he didn't come home and then crawled in next morning, all scented and half dead. . . ." He had turned half away, and looking at his face she saw for the first time a kind of beauty in it that neutralized her own sharp disgust. It was not the perversity of his life but its messiness that had repelled her. Now she understood with surprise that he was suffering, and the quality he had most needed, his dignity, again fitted around him.

Wasn't it better to be alone? But then you dried up. She found she liked Giles now better than before. Before he had never offered himself as a subject for any feeling.

They went to Fatehpur Sikri in the morning. Helen would have preferred the Taj Mahal, but Indra, making laws for the weekend, said there was to be no splitting up. With all her cosmopolitan dash—her cropped hair and blue matador trousers—when it came to picnics she was wholly Indian and wanted them as large as possible, noisy, late to start and well supplied with food. She snatched up four bemused American tourists who were staying at the hotel and helplessly waiting for Agra to find them, wedged Helen between Lakshmi and Otto in the back of their own car and off they went.

They allowed themselves to be taken in hand by a guide. Submission seemed the best course, better than the mean, shrill fight for independence. The guide knew next to nothing and could not impart what little knowledge he had, but at least he offered protection from other guides.

They followed him over the sunburnt courts. It was getting toward noon and their shadows dropped short and black behind them. The new Americans asked endless questions. They had been in India for only four days and were still struck with surprise by anomalies that confronted them like evil gods, staring down with menace on their Christian souls. Was it true that a Brahman would not drink water from an Untouchable's well, even if he happened to be dying of thirst? Was it true that if your shadow passed over him when he was eating, he had to throw the food away and take a bath?

Helen dropped back with Otto, knowing that she would not have to talk to him. He moved beside her, loose and slow-footed like an animal, with his heavy plotting eyes on the back of Krishan's neck. Krishan was excited and mischievous. He ran and played with the children, becoming, for their entertainment, twelve years old. He seemed to be performing to an audience and atoning for something. Helen saw him press close to Giles, touching the back of his hand with his fingertips.

"You are not still angry? It was a joke. Nobody understands me when I am teasing. Where is your sense of humor?"

"Miriam House," said the guide. "Astrologer's seat. . . . Salim Chishti's tomb."

Holy unkempt men with avaricious eyes squatted in the doorways, presiding expensively over the shoes of visitors. Sunlight fell through the pierced screens, throwing a filigree of gold on the marble floor. Helen, who was not afraid to admire the obvious, preferred marble to sandstone, and thought the saint's tomb very beautiful. But the rest of Fatehpur Sikri did not move her. The city seemed not so much deserted by life as never infused with it. Though five centuries old, it had known only twelve years of history and been abandoned on its completion. There were no tales to tell of valor and treachery, of murdered fathers and mad imprisoned sons. Even time had left it untouched, as though the centuries laid no claim to it. Too sharp, too fresh, it was as clean as an architectural drawing, like the imitation of an ancient city, with everything, except age, exactly reproduced.

She walked across the court to the outside wall. On the brown plain below, two white bullocks, their eyes blinded with leather pads, turned a water-wheel; a woman crossed a field, carrying three brass pots in a tower on her head. Helen sat down, leaning with her back against the wall, and held out her legs to the sun. She was thinking of Krishan and Giles, and wondered why it was that other people's love looked ugly when hers looked beautiful. The question did not trouble her for long, or lead her into any close self-analysis. She simply said to herself, "Because it's different."

By midafternoon they were driving back, dodging the cycles and bullock carts, and the rickety garis with their bright polished brass and moth-eaten plumes.

At the hotel they had tea; then Giles wanted to visit an antique shop and look at Mogul paintings.

"I'll come with you," said Helen, suddenly deciding to buy me a gift. She knew exactly what she wanted: one of those small brass figures of the Hindu gods—Ganesha, the fat little elephant god. I had told her once that he was the god of obstacles.

"You can drive us, Krishan."

Krishan was eating his third piece of cake. "It's just down the road," he said. "Can't you walk?" When Giles glared at him he looked up sulkily. "I am tired and I have to drive all the way home."

To Helen's surprise Indra supported him. "Leave the boy alone, Giles. Let him rest."

The antique shop was a long bungalow set back within an uncared-for garden. Children and pye-dogs had trodden the lawn to dust. Within, a darker dust coated the dubious treasures.

Giles argued over a Rajput painting with the Jain proprietor; a yellow-eyed man with a betel-stained mouth. Helen looked for her gift amongst a collection of little gnome-like brass figures, humble household versions of gods who had dropped their more splendid attributes to serve the smaller side of human nature. . . . Let me pass my examination. . . . Let my wife be beautiful and fair. . . . Let me make a lot of money. . . .

She had her choice from fifteen Ganeshas and instinctively

picked one that had little beauty but looked, by the wear upon it, to have seen the most of life and prayer.

Indra called out from the doorway, "Giles, we are going now. It's after five."

He was still annoyed with her for supporting Krishan and said in a high, spiteful voice, "What! You an Indian, and the first to start. You're out of character. You ought to be keeping us all hanging around and wondering if it's worth it."

But she only laughed. "It's not me. It's Don. He has been working hard for the past half hour getting me ready."

Giles looked intently at his painting.

"Aren't you coming then?"

"Soon."

"Then we'll go on. You'll have to take Otto. He and Krishan are still having tea."

All the way back to the hotel he muttered under his breath.

"You wait around for them half your life. . . ."

"It's a conspiracy. . . ."

"Only bazaar painting. Bloody rogues all fakes."

At the hotel gate he suddenly fell silent. The chairs on the veranda were empty. Sparrows pecked at crumbs of cake on the tray. Giles hurried away to his room.

Helen waited for the three men by the car. They all arrived together, as though they had met somewhere else, and their blank, unconcerned faces looked severely determined against any admission of how or where. Otto got into the back beside Helen. As they drove out from the city, the peasants were coming in off the fields and the road was a clutter of bullock carts, bicycles and tongas. Even the sky was thick with crows coming in to their roosts in the Agra trees." They flew low down in a black, slow stream, heading, it would seem, straight into the windshield of the car, and then, like hedgehopping planes, lifting up to flap over the hood.

Krishan, who when they left the hotel had been sulky and quiet, suddenly plunged into one of his playful moods. He began teasing the traffic, honking and shouting at the carts and bullying the cyclists off the road. He kept lifting his eyes to the rear-vision mirror and throwing his reflected smiles into the back of the car.

"See, I nearly hit him! Look! He's fallen off!"

The cyclist wobbled drunkenly and turned his front wheel into a ditch.

Giles said crisply, "If you don't behave I won't let you drive the car at all."

Krishan slammed on the brakes so sharply that Helen plunged forward against the front seat. He turned off the ignition and threw his hands in the air. "All right! Then I won't drive. *You* drive!" He turned around, leaning his chin on his hands. "He hates driving," he told Otto gaily. "He's all the time frightened he's going to hit something. I drive very well. I can miss by a bee's knee. Mrs. Siegel, don't you think I am a good driver?"

"Would you like me to drive for a while?" said Otto, leaning forward and speaking to Krishan in a low voice.

"I'll thank you," said Giles, "not to interfere with my domestic staff. You can drive on," he said to Krishan, "or get out and walk." Krishan had pushed him back into his old self. He was not going to discuss anything but simply sat with folded arms, in silence. Helen was glad. She had not enjoyed seeing Giles without his dignity. She preferred him light, cruel and vain, cracking other people like nuts between his teeth. Sulkily Krishan started the car again.

They drove on in silence through the closing dark. At about

eight o'clock, and still thirty miles from Delhi, they came on the Bradens, pulled up by the side of the road. Don stepped forward, waving his arms.

"What's the matter?" Giles called out.

"I don't know. I can't see. Have you got a torch?"

Giles found a torch in the front pocket. He got out and went across to the other car. Indra, thermos in hand, was pouring tea into red plastic cups, and the children unwrapped bundles of sandwiches.

"Do you want some tea? There are still some sandwiches." She looked vivid and gay. Anything that happened was all to the good, providing it presented an opportunity to eat.

Giles and Don leaned over the hood—dark shapes with ruddy, lit-up faces, like fortune-tellers.

Helen put her hand on the door to open it, then heard Krishan's laugh bubbling out. In the next moment they were hurtling down the road.

"What are you *doing?*"

Simultaneously Otto cried out, "Stop! You silly little fool!" But Krishan laughed and laughed, increasing his speed.

Otto leaned forward and put his hands lightly on Krishan's shoulders. "You must go back," he said gently. "This is ridiculous, you must go back!"

"Why? What does it matter? He can go with the others. It serves him right!"

"He will be furious with you. This is his car. You will make him mad."

"It's a joke! It's a bloody damned good joke! We shall be home first. I hope it takes them a jolly long time to get that old cart going!" He was delighted with what he was doing, but already frightened, and driving away faster and faster became not only a joke but an escape from consequences.

"Speak to him, Helen!"

"It's no good," said Helen. And suddenly she began to think, clearly and quickly, about her life as she was now going to lead it. It was as though Krishan's spontaneous, reckless act had released a stoppage in her consciousness. The speed at which they were traveling made her feel that time was precious. Any decisions that had to be made had to be made now.

She saw her marriage with Fred, a partnership forged for other people's reasons, almost as though she herself had not been consulted. Young girls got married in that Victorian backwater, that left-behind world, with its homely virtues and simple stipulations. Young girls did get married—marriage was the social law—and she and Fred had stamped passports for each other. But that was all past. The snap choice, the tolerant affection, the mediocrity—with the best of life lived alone. Even when he loved her, still alone . . . her arms wrapped around him, while he tucked his infant knees into her belly and took her breast like a dummy into his mouth. The mother goddess—succoring, supporting, alleviating a moment's desirous distress—but without any desires or needs of her own. Until now. And now no one was going to take anything from her.

Passion does not last—older, more experienced friends had assured her. She was prepared to believe what they said. It sounded wise, and it was unimportant.

I'm sorry, Fred. I'm sorry! He would be very hurt, but he'd get over it. His affections flowed thinly; she had never felt herself saturated, only a little damp, as in a light shower; and it was in his pride that he would be hurt, not in his heart. She did not think less of him for that. Suffering is suffering, and wherever it happens to lodge, the sensation is the same.

The trees fled past, and the long straight road, known to the feet of princes and emperors, peasants, naked sadhus, goats, cows.

Krishan swerved and honked his horn. The bullock cart ahead pulled slowly over to the right. He had also pulled over to pass it on that side and had to swerve quickly across, his left front tire skidding on the gravel off the road. Helen caught a glimpse of the docile beasts, their gentle heads dipping up and down, and their milk-white skins shifting about like silk on their big, sharp bones. She heard a knock, and felt a faint jar as they struck the edge of the cart. The peasant, high up on his load of fodder, waved his staff and shouted.

Otto cried out from the back, "You are driving *too fast!*" Krishan put on his brakes, but too late, and Helen flung her hands up over her face. A second driver, hearing the warning horn, had drawn his animals over to the left. His cart was loaded with long dipping sheaves of cut bamboo. They plunged toward the windshield like spears.

There were moments when Helen knew nothing, only bearing with her through darkness the sensation of a world overturned, the shocking fracture of everything that was whole. She saw buildings falling, and great rocks opening in jagged splits.

When she opened her eyes, it was to look up into a sky dripping with leaves. Something was crawling on the back of her hand. This was all she could feel—no soreness, no pain; her body might have been paralyzed. Only her hand flinched back from the trespass of a small unseen creature. Then whatever it was bit her, and a needle-sharp pain sang in her palm.

It acted upon her like a stimulant, making her conscious of the overturned car, the smell of gasoline, the shouting. She began to crawl away, found that she was bruised and in pain, but that she could crawl. Her head reeled, and the earth dipped and swayed like water sloshing back and forth in a basin. Something white shuddered before her eyes; then her vision cleared and she saw the head of a cow. It lay with its long white cheek pressed to the earth, and a soft dreadful sound came from its mouth; its black nostrils, like bellows, beat out and in, and its belly and haunches lifted and fell in big convulsive movements.

Later, the scene had to be interpreted for her. The fallen cow, its side impaled with a splintered shaft; the other animal struggling to rise and pulling its wounded partner with it, so that even though the cow was half dead it heaved and jerked with a grotesque and terrible semblance of protest and power.

The peasants did nothing to help the suffering animals but moaned with grief at their loss, and howled with rage for the insult to their faith. Helen lay with their feet stamping senselessly about her, their brown naked legs and flapping dhotis filling the darkness with an impression of turmoil and panic.

They found Otto dead—his chest had been pierced by one of the bamboo stakes. Krishan moaned. They hauled him out and clubbed him to death. Then they saw Helen move as, finding a fresh area of pain down her thigh, she rolled over on her back.

They stood gigantically above her; tall Punjabis with lean, straight bodies and turbaned heads. They looked like giants. When they lifted up their arms, the points of their staves seemed to touch the stars. They did not beat her face or her body, perhaps because she was a woman, but with all the power of their bitter sorrow and rage they smashed the long shafts on her wrists and legs.

"Human beings in India," Giles said, "comprise one-sixth of the world's population, but there are two hundred and twenty-five million cattle—one-*quarter* of the cattle in the world. Throughout the East there is an unsatisfied demand for cattle carcasses, which sell at one hundred dollars per piece. If India were to sell eighty million cattle carcasses, she could earn four billion dollars in foreign exchange."

He claimed that these figures came from an F.A.O. report. He had become very interested in India's cow problem.

"Last year in Gujarat," he told me, "twenty per cent of the calves starved to death. It's not worth while keeping a calf going, because it doesn't start producing for a year. Old cows don't starve. They have learned to live on rags and dust, pieces of galvanized iron—if there's any about—sticks and thorns. Who knows, perhaps they are carnivorous? In any case they don't starve; they simply fade away. Or else they are eaten. Not by people, of course.

"Driving along the Ring Road the other day, I saw an old cow—terribly, terribly old and terribly sick—it could hardly stand. Two crows, sitting on its back, ate it. They had got right through the skin and were down onto the bone. When they stuck their beaks in for another bite, you could see that the red holes were about two inches deep and, I should say, about four inches in diameter.

"I stopped and got out of my car. You wouldn't believe it. It takes a lot to whip me into indignation. I shouted and shooed them away—but of course they came back. Who's going to leave a big, fat, walking meal like that? And so *fresh!* I said to myself, 'There goes God, no less.' "

The cow on the Agra road, which was God too, had been about four years old, in Giles' opinion. Well fed, strong, in its prime. He had studied it closely. He had had plenty of time.

It had taken them half an hour to get the car going. And when they came upon the accident, the peasants had cut the live animal loose and had gone. Giles and the others stood appalled by a disaster that seemed too large for them to deal with. The children screamed and broke into loud weeping and Indra turned away from the broken, contorted bodies of Krishan and Otto. Helen lay with her eyes wide open and smiled at them, but her consciousness ebbed far behind her smile, and later she did not remember having seen them. They could not bear to look at her shattered leg. Her arm below the elbow looked shapeless, soggy and wet, like crushed fruit. They were thirty miles from Delhi.

"I made them go on," said Giles, "and I waited."

His courage surprised me and I wondered if he knew what courage had been needed. The peasants might have come back; others might have followed after. The unspeakable crime remained—the broken cart and the sacred, murdered body.

It was three hours before the ambulance arrived, and carts did pass, but they crossed to the other side of the road and did not stop. Three hours of darkness and solitude, with the jackals coming up to the smell of blood.

He said in a dry voice, "Someone had to watch over him."

Chapter Sixteen

IT WAS NOT AN INDIAN HOSPITAL. AMERICANS AND EUROPEANS ran it and provided its senior medical staff, but as I approached it I was overwhelmingly conscious that it was *in* India, and that this was an all-conditioning fact, impinging on the sternest Western concepts.

In a stall that had been set up by the gate, lethargic young men repaired radio sets and bicycles. Old tires hung like bangles on the broken arms of trees; valves, tubes, screws littered the floor. They knew their business, these pavement mechanics, and machines were made to work again—if not in the way their makers had intended. There is plenty of reparation in a country where so much is broken, and damaged human beings had been put together in the same offhand way. An old man showed a blind silver eye; a child dragged a crippled foot.

I walked up through the neat petunia beds, and the mallee, tending his plants, dribbled water from the belly of a dead goat in the manner of the past two thousand years.

And because it was India I could bully my way past gentle, ill-trained nurses, who softly gave way to my look of authority.

It wasn't a bad room, though not what you would call quiet, with the bicycle bells twanging outside in the road and the pavement radios blaring. They had drawn the curtains against the glare of light shaking up off the red gravel drive, and she lay in the half dark, looking small, like a child.

I had an impression of a body painstakingly, meticulously bandaged, as though it had been broken into a dozen pieces and stuck together about an undamaged trunk and small, wracked face. When she saw me she smiled; then tears welled up and slipped down out of the sides of her eyes. I leaned down and kissed her, holding my cheek against hers. It was all I could do to stop myself from weeping too.

"Damn! Blast!" She couldn't stop crying and her weakness made her angry, because, as she explained to me later, she didn't feel too bad now and she wasn't at all unhappy.

"They've doped me to the eyebrows. It makes you feel so weak and stupid." She turned her head from side to side. "Don't look at me. It's ridiculous! I just bloody well can't stop sniveling."

My feelings were simple and bold; they beat within me like drums. I felt such grief for her I would have borne all she suffered for myself; and a tenderness that seemed to wash back upon my spirit, so that I was happier than I had ever been in my life.

I felt a curious awe for what had happened. I saw it for more than it was, as though it were something that concerned us both and was a product of what we had felt for each other. This was not the trivial domestic drama that Helen had feared; we had struck the right note. Events had lent us dignity and made us look fine in each other's eyes. They seemed to confirm our beliefs, to thrust us forward into what we wanted to do. We felt a security we had not felt before, as though our hesitations, all the arguments that spoke against us, had shriveled up in the glare of this brutal happening.

Her right leg was the problem, it turned out. It was broken in three places. Not just broken—shattered, crushed. Even the best doctor might not have been good enough; and in India, as in Mandalay, "the best is like the worst"—a fact which occasionally appalls us, but perhaps it is we Westerners who are unwise. We have lost our old casual faith—"He will come . . . soon . . . tomorrow . . . she will get better . . . yes, yes." We have taken over the purposes of the Almighty (as Giles would say), and we get down to details all the time. Dr. Aziz's collar stud was given to a friend, and this is a good reason for not having one— but it is only one of a hundred reasons that India makes by way of excuse, and behind them all persists the belief that collar studs really do not matter.

Her leg did mend, but an inch shorter than the left one, and with a look of woody straightness from ankle to knee. For years to come, small splinters of bone worked through the skin.

Krishan's body had been returned to his family. Otto's funeral had taken place that morning. Fresh from tragedy, I saw, or thought I saw, with a clearer vision; so that was a unique occasion. Later it all looked different. But that difference was something I had to be shown.

As the days passed I spent more time with Helen. I got up at six-thirty, leaving Pamela asleep, and went out to the College at eight. Then at ten-thirty I drove back into Delhi and sat with her for an hour in the morning. Later, other visitors came; and

Fern Chase, finding me there, began to look critical. It was not the time for straightening out misunderstandings, but there was no confusion any more between what was important and what was not.

Hilton still hadn't been able to find Fred. Later that week he rang me up.

"Dick, we've just had a cable from New York. They can't locate him."

"It doesn't matter. You've done all you can."

"But, Dick, he *ought* to know."

"She says it would worry him. Illness is his privilege. If she gets sick he has very quickly to get sicker. He would have to think up something pretty good to do better than this, wouldn't he?"

"Don't be so bitter, Dick. Fred is a really nice guy. I guess you don't care for him too much, but he really *is* a nice guy. After all, he doesn't know she's had this smash. Now, you can't blame him for that, can you?"

"No." But I did blame him. His silence, his continued absence, further belittled him. He was nothing now.

Pamela lay on her bed with her eyes closed. After the first glance I sat down and opened a file I had brought with me. I knew what I was expected to have noticed: the look of exhaustion, the drawn brows, that meant a headache—coming or going. A bottle of Disprin stood on the table by her bed. But Pamela's little miseries had shriveled beside the catastrophe to Helen, and I turned away, leaving her to her good health and her sound constitution.

Twelve years ago, her present disposition had shown as no more than a shadow on her nature: occasional moods, becoming imperceptibly less occasional, until now they had all but swallowed up the light, sane episodes of her life—her sense of humor, her gaiety—had even eaten away her prettiness.

"Oh, you're back. I didn't hear you come in."

"Didn't you?"

"Where have you been?"

"I went to see Helen Siegel."

"I do think it's good of you. She must be very grateful."

"I knew them quite well."

"Have they found the husband yet?"

"I don't think so."

"It must be terrible for her. Strong healthy people who are never sick just can't understand what it's like. . . . I woke up this morning feeling so happy, and now this headache . . . I've had it all the afternoon. I feel so depressed I could just lie down and cry."

"Well, you are lying down. All you need to do is cry."

"What did you say?"

"Nothing."

"I thought you spoke."

I knew what was asked of me, but I could not move. I had discovered in myself a power for cruelty that awed me. "You've been in all day," I said pleasantly. "You ought to try and get some exercise."

"What and where?"

"You could swim. You could play tennis, golf, ping-pong, badminton, or you could ride."

"All alone . . ."

"You can always go for a walk."

"In this country! The moment you set foot outside the gate a horde of vile filthy children pester you for money."

"Well then, we're not left with much, are we? Would you like me to take you for a drive?"

That night, all else having failed, she came and lay down beside me on my bed, offering her magnanimous and unrejoicing body for me to use. Soft at first, and turned to fit my thigh, and then, when I did not move, becoming rigid and hard. She lay on her back with her legs straight and joined, like an image carved on a sarcophagus. Spasms of trembling seized her.

I said, "Are you cold?"

"No, I'm not cold. I'm not cold. *Darling.* You seem so strange, so far away. So *hard* . . ." Her whisper came from the very nadir of abnegation. There was nothing further to give up and no rescue except from me. So I turned and put my arms around her, holding her limply against my body. But I couldn't speak to her or caress her. I might have been holding a stone.

The consequences of our acts are forever part of us and for years now I had told myself that she was my own creation, her sufferings and her selfishness nurtured by my protective love. But now this sense of an unrejectable obligation seemed like an attitude of mind that could be put away as one puts away one's thoughts. Feeling the vacancy between us, the absence of any tenderness, she pulled herself from my arms and stumbled to her bed.

I lay, calmly, listening to her crying. But you can't go on crying all alone. There's really no point. So silence came. Then I heard her unscrewing the cap from her bottle of sleeping pills.

Sikh children played cricket in the compound, using a tree shield as a wicket—there was no tree inside it—and a broken plank of wood as a bat. The windows of Shankar's flat seemed to be shuttered, and no red eiderdown hung from the balcony.

I said to the tallest child, "Can you tell me what has happened to Shankar Dhas? Has he gone away?"

He answered in English learned at school, and getting farther and farther from its living sources. "Sir, that man has gone away. He is no longer residing in his abode."

"When did he go?"

"Tomorrow."

"Do you mean yesterday?"

"Has gone. Will not come back," he said sulkily. No assurance here; he gave me a dark, hostile look. With his father—possibly a shopkeeper, more probably an Army man—I would have felt an immediate bond. We had met in history and walked two hundred years of it together; love and hate swung between us, back and forth, and often we were closer than closer kin—neighbors over the border, cousins across the sea. But in one generation the bonds had been cut.

I had never been inside Shankar's office, but I knew where it was—just beyond Harding Bridge, on a corner where four roads converged. A newly developed area, still without trees; bare, and hazy with dust. New Government buildings rose out of it haphazardly and the plots between were a slum of open drains and workmen's huts.

A doorman in a brown coat wore a large brass badge to announce his function. I asked not for Shankar but for Dr. Batterjee. We walked down a corridor spattered with betel stains. Peons squatted outside open doors, presiding over towers of files tied up with pieces of dirty tape. A woman crouched against the wall, breast-feeding a baby.

Dr. Batterjee had his office to himself, and sat on a chair behind a desk. He had a dark, heavy face that was not bearded, and not clean-shaven either, but maintained an indeterminate position somewhere between the hairy and the smooth. He wore a long, tight sherwani that was torn at the elbows and had lost two buttons. He rose to his feet when I came in and told a peon to get me a chair.

"Sir, to what do I owe this pleasure? What can I do for you?"

I touched the soft, unresponsive hand. "I wondered if you could tell me where I can find Shankar Dhas."

"Ah!" He put his hands together, placing the fingertips gently against one another, and moved his head from side to side. "Won't you sit down?"

"I went to his house," I said, "and it's shut up. They couldn't tell me where he had gone."

We were both seated now. He leaned his elbows on the littered desk. Shankar had spoken well of him and I was prepared to like him. He looked a strong, calm man. He also looked ill. The whites of his eyes were the color of nicotine, their expression remote and melancholy.

"I think your name is Richard Mardellis. He has told me about you."

"We talked on the telephone. You told me not to trust in mechanical inventions."

"That is true," he said gravely. "It is the error of modern man. We should return for inspiration to the insects and the rocks."

"But when Columbus discovered America, Dr. Batterjee, he couldn't very well pretend that it wasn't there."

"Ah! You are right. Always there are these obstacles of truth all about us. You know your friend has suffered a great sorrow. Who can step into a brother's place? We are resigned to the loss of father, mother; but a brother should be a companion throughout life. It seems he fell into the hands of a bad man."

"He was his own worst enemy."

"Ah, and is that not so of all of us? The truth comes out of your mouth. I see you are a wise man—it is a privilege to share your thoughts. Your friend is not here. He has gone back to his village."

"You mean he's resigned?"

"No, he has not resigned. At times like this we seek our dear ones, isn't it?" His hot, sad eyes looked into mine. "How he loved you, sir, like a brother. Often he has told me about you. 'What a man!' he has said, 'and how happy I would be if you could meet him!' Now I have had this happiness and I understand what this friendship meant to him. He said to me the day he left, 'If my friend should come to see me, tell him my thoughts are with him. Tell him of my loyalty and my devotion.'"

"He said that?"

Dr. Batterjee lifted his hand and quickly flicked his wrist, as though shaking water from his fingertips. "They were his exact words. I swear it."

I have often since looked back on this curious conversation and tried to find some meaning in it, searched it for irony and then for compassion. But I can come to no conclusion about it, and its meaning changes depending on my mood—whether of anger, affection or remorse.

Chapter Seventeen

TWO DAYS AFTER MY VISIT TO DR. BATTERJEE, A STRONG HOT wind raked the city from the west, and the sky all around the horizon wore dust like a nimbus of smoke; only directly overhead the struggling blue gained a mild supremacy. Tombs and mosques which had once been beautiful looked squat and ugly—half their size—cowering down under the sky's brown shoulder. I remember thinking, This is the first day of summer.

I left my car outside the U.N. Office, and as I crossed the compound, dust skidded away before my feet in clots and streaks, halting here and there to writhe and twist, like some mean, ugly animal that drags its belly on the ground.

Hilton greeted me with "Richard, we've just heard from Fred. He cabled from San Francisco. He's canceled his trip to Paris—"

"I don't believe it."

"And he'll be arriving at ten-thirty tonight."

"Tonight!"

The news shocked me—Fred had begun to seem shadowy—then I felt resentful, as though he had no right to return suddenly like this, just when it suited him. It was a typical piece of callous selfishness, this out-of-the-blue announcement of his return.

Hilton said, "There's no mention of Helen. What do you think, Dick? I guess he doesn't know. He can't have received our cables to New York."

I read the cable. "Arriving seventeenth, ten-thirty P.A.A. Flight 721."

"Perhaps he's saving money."

He blinked his gray eyes quickly as though to rid them of the grit of my cynicism. "I'm glad you came, Dick. I was going to phone you. Sir Malcolm's having a reception tonight for those scientific congress guys. I was wondering if you could go to the airport and meet Fred."

"What, no transport for Fred Siegel?" I mocked him.

But doggedly he thought the best of me. "We have to pick the delegates up at their hotel and take them back. You know we're very short of transport, Dick."

"Don't worry. I'll meet him." I said after a pause, "Does Helen know?"

"Sure she knows. Fern's out at the hospital now. This is a relief, Dick. It sure does take a weight off my mind."

Along King's Way the flags were out—a line of crimson tongues, licking the wind—and banners flapped and cracked on rocking poles. Some Russian V.I.P. was arriving that afternoon.

I didn't want to go back to the hotel, and drove aimlessly, choosing my way on an impulse at each intersection. I told myself that I wanted to think, but I thought of nothing. I felt a curious dread and, overlying it, a numbness that affected even my sense of my love for Helen. I was living, like an Indian, on hope. Everything will be all right; everything will come to a happy end. . . . But there was one all-important factor I was refusing to see, and I felt that unease we always know when we shut ourselves away in the temporary security of self-deception.

On the veranda I passed Alisulman, hurrying along with a coil of rope. The mallee squatted on the steps, sticking flowers into trumpet-shaped brass vases, and one of Soni's relations, who did odd jobs about the place, stood on a ladder fixing up a string of colored globes. I remembered then that Soni was giving a party that evening and that Pamela and I had been invited to it. I opened the door thinking that we would at least have a subject for conversation.

She stood in the center of the room, facing me, and I had the impression that she had been standing like this for a long time, waiting for the door to open. She swore at me—three words that sounded dreadful and filthy, because I had never heard her use them before.

She opened her mouth again and her jaw worked up and down, but no sound came. I said quickly, "When you've pulled yourself together I'll listen to you."

I went into the bathroom and turned on the tap by the washbasin. My heart thudded, and I felt nauseated under the sudden strain on my body, so that I leaned my hands on the basin for a moment and hung dizzily over it. I knew that something I had always dreaded was about to happen. Then I washed my hands and dried them carefully, praying to hear the sound of her crying. Tense with fear, I went back into the other room.

She was sitting on the bed, her hand over her eyes. I sweated with relief and said to her gently, "Now, tell me what's happened."

She put her hand in the neck of her dress and pulled out a letter. She gave it to me, keeping her head turned away and her hand like a shield over her eyes. It was such a theatrical gesture I began to doubt the sincerity of whatever feeling she was trying to show me. And then I read that extraordinary letter that Shankar wrote to my wife.

I read it only once. Later—in the afternoon, or perhaps that evening—Pamela destroyed it. And that also poses an interesting question. Was she afraid that someone else might see it? Was she sparing me, or herself? I can't believe that she wanted to spare me anything, so perhaps she was obliterating evidence of her own humiliation. Or did she guess that I might want to come back to it and search it again for some mitigating thought? Or was it just the beginning of the demolition—a little fire to start the whole thing off?

In any case I read it only once, and I still don't know whether those astounding words were not partly my own imagination.

DEAR PAMELA,

It was very good and kind of you to write to me. I feel this gesture shows the generosity of your nature and an understanding for other people which I remarked when I first met you. It distresses me that I did not meet you again. I did not even know that you had returned to New Delhi. Richard has now entirely discontinued his visits to me, otherwise he would have brought you with him. . . .

"I didn't know you wrote to him."

She muttered into her hand, "I thought I knew *you*."

Your letter came to me at a time of great suffering and for this reason it carried a power to comfort. It does comfort me and it will be your hand that I touch when I want to show friendliness to your people.

His duty, he told her, had been revealed in prayer. Reciprocity: kindness for kindness shown. And the greatest gift we have to offer one another is Truth. Affection can turn upon us and eat our flesh. Love attaches to the world and all its sorrow. So out came Truth: pages and pages of Truth, all about me. It was important that Pamela should know me, in Shankar's view. For reasons somewhat obscure. At the beginning of this extraordinary catalogue he advised caution. Know your situation and beware. Roll in pitch, and pitch will cover your skin. . . . Later on he slipped into another mood and seemed to feel that she might help in my salvation.

For I loved him once, he said, but grew to hate him. Why? No reason given, or was there? I seem to remember something about Shankar having lied to me. To revenge myself upon him, I deliberately corrupted and ruined his brother, driving him in the end to a terrible death. A boy still not formed. I tempted him with material luxury and handed him over for the uses of an evil man. Giles, in return, fed my sexual appetite by procuring me women. Young virgins, married women, I took them to his flat and seduced them there, and Giles further degraded Krishan's young mind by pouring into his ears tales of my lasciviousness.

I said, "God knows how he knew about this." And yet I could visualize clearly how it had happened. Shankar lecturing Krishan on the dangers of his new easy life and Krishan contemptuous, on top of the world, laughing at Shankar's Puritan fears: "Look at your wonderful friend! That's the kind of man you admire. . . ."

"Then it's true!"

"Of course it's not *true!* It's utterly, stupidly, fantastically wrong! 'Remember me to him and guard him with your affection. He is dear to me. . . .' He's out of his mind! He doesn't know what he's saying!"

"You mean you never had those women . . . and then this Helen Siegel. No wonder you've been such a ministering angel. She has so *few* friends. Her husband's away. . . . My God!"

"Yes, that's true, but not how he talks about it. Pamela, you've know all along that I've had other women. It was the only possible way. And it never happened when you were there. Would you have preferred it if I'd told you about it?"

"I don't know." She put up her hands again and began to shudder.

"Stop it!" I said to her sharply. "It's absolutely stupid going on like this just because a half-crazy man writes an insane letter and tells you something you already know."

"*I didn't know anything about Helen Siegel!*" she screamed at me.

"Well, you know now."

"*You killed that boy!*"

"Pull yourself together. You're hysterical. You're worse than Shankar."

"You'll kill me next! You don't want me. I know. . . ."

I said, "Well, that makes it easier, doesn't it?"

"Makes what easier?"

"Facing the fact that we can't go on living together."

"*Richard!*"

"I'm sorry. It was bound to happen sometime. You and I haven't had any sort of relationship now for years. We're just eating each other alive. I expect it's my fault as much as yours.

But it doesn't do any good apportioning blame, because it's too late now. And you'll be better off too."

"Here he goes saying 'You'll be better off too.' My God, how right Shankar was!"

I got up.

"Where are you going?"

"I'm going to Helen."

"Richard! I warn you. . . ."

"What do you mean?" I spoke to her gently but coldly. I believed I had no feeling for her, either of resentment or affection. I just wanted her once and for all to understand. "I love her and I'm going to marry her . . . if we can. If we can't, we'll live together. I've been through half my life. I believe I'm entitled to some normal, ordinary happiness. You're perfectly capable of living without me if you try."

"*Richard!*"

I opened the door. I expected her to scream out again, but she didn't. And when I closed the door the room was silent behind me.

Out on the veranda I paused, wondering what to do now. As though there were anything that could now be done. I was like a traveler who stubbornly says "I shall embark tomorrow" when the ship is on fire.

I was conscious of there being nowhere to go. I couldn't go in to lunch, because Pamela might decide to take lunch too and it seemed positively unsafe to risk another meeting until the sediment of the last scene had dropped. So no lunch—at any rate, not here—and I couldn't see Helen till four. I walked to my car, and a phrase from Shankar's letter beat through my mind. "He destroys everything he touches. . . ." Had Shankar said that? Surely he couldn't possibly have written that! Then I thought that I wanted to go back to my room and get the letter from Shankar and read it again. And that I couldn't do this either.

The wind threw a flurry of leaves over the lawn. The handle of the car when I touched it was burning hot.

"Sir!"

A young man stepped from behind the car. His shirt hung outside his trousers and over this he wore a long frayed coat, buttoned tightly across a chest so narrow I could have spanned it with my hands. He stood staring at me with large, protuberant eyes and swallowed, so that the pointed Adam's apple jumped up and down in his throat. He said, "You will give me money!"

"Money?" I stupidly repeated.

He pulled a sheaf of dirty papers from his pocket and pressed them into my hands. I looked down and I knew without reading them more or less what they would say—stiff, impersonal pronouncements from men and women who when it came to the point could not speak out with heartless honesty. If you emptied out all India's pockets, how many of these futile and untruthful testimonials would you find? Giles, I thought, with his passion for statistics, might have been interested to know.

. . . Intelligent but lacks practical ability. . . . Sincere, intelligent . . . shows an interest in his work but lacks application. . . .

"You will give me a hundred rupees," he said. "I am a poor student. You will pay for my education."

I took out my wallet. It contained eighty rupees. I kept ten and put seventy into his outstretched hand. Heaven knows what impelled me. He looked the most unworthy object for charity, and I have never before felt an impulse to such undisciplined largess.

He was so surprised he didn't even thank me; but not too surprised to press his advantage. His eyes fell to the ten-rupee note in my hand. I gave him this too. How mighty are the poor with their ineradicable pathos and insatiable demands; and what power they have over the strong and rich, whose only longing is to escape them. But how do you escape? Through indifference, through cruelty, through the death of your own soul? If he had only known, he had me now. I was totally at his mercy. I would have given him my shirt if he had asked for it.

"Sahib. . . ."

So we were back again in the old paternal days! The word let me go. After all that, he was going to be grateful. I got quickly into the car and started the engine up before the scene could expand and grow soft and messy.

I was out of the gate when I realized that now I had no money, and that I had to eat and drink and get through the rest of the day till I picked up Fred. It seemed extraordinary to be thinking about such trivial matters, but cautions rooted in more prosaic times had me turning the car and driving back to the hotel.

I stopped outside the kitchens and sneaked along the veranda, so as not to meet the object of my charity. So as not to meet Pamela.

I saw myself doing this and it seemed so ridiculous I began to laugh. "He destroys everything he touches. . . ." According to Shankar, I had even destroyed a morsel of India. I accepted a large allowance out of the poor squeezed coffers of the Indian Government and instead of working I went off and slept with women. I was as bad as Fred. And not only did I do no work—the noble, important work of alleviating the miseries of the most distressed people on earth—I was actually contemptuous of the work I was meant to be doing. "It's all a waste of time and money," I said. Shouldn't I have been accorded the virtue of honesty? Well, apparently not. Because everything is right and well done, and we are all going to be better off in the end. The poor will be rich, the hungry will eat. . . . Yes, yes. . . .

But at least I had done something to further the education of a poor student. Or given him a good meal. Or a pair of silver bangles for his wife.

Agawalla was in his office. He took his naked feet off the table and shuffled them back into his sandals. It was the beginning of summer. Flies moved about a dirty teacup. A new dirty teacup—though still an old one. It was white with a chip, but no crack. The other one had had a crack but no chip.

"Sir, what can I do for you?"

"Can you cash me a check, Agawalla? The banks are shut and I haven't any money."

"Mr. Mardellis, I am very sorry, but Mr. Soni has the keys to the safe and he is not here." He put his hand in his pocket and took out three indescribably dirty ten-rupee notes. "Let me lend you this."

He too recognized the virtue of giving. His face shone with happiness as the grace of God dropped like rain on his soul. He was lucky. He was giving his thirty rupees to a man who did not need them, who would pay them back tomorrow and go away.

Her cheek had the damp, rubbery feel that our flesh takes on when it's fighting. "You're not well. Is your leg still aching?"

"No, not at all. I don't feel anything." Her smile looked tight and forced. "Except in the behind where they're pumping me with penicillin."

Outside the wind still raked the trees. Dust hung in the air, bringing the sky close; it was turning a violet pink, like rotten fruit. "It's nothing to worry about," she said. "You know how they adore penicillin."

"Have you heard about Fred?"

"Yes, Fern was here this morning."

"I'm going to pick him up at the airport."

"I know."

I said, "Have you got any money in your bag? I had to borrow thirty rupees from Agawalla and I've already spent twenty."

"I did have something, but they took my things away. Why did you have to borrow from Agawalla?"

"I gave eighty rupees to an Indian student who wanted a weekend in Bombay and a new silk sari for his wife."

"You're kidding. That doesn't sound like you."

"He told me I ought to pay for his education. I thought God might reward me."

"Do you believe in God? I ought to know that sort of thing."

"I do now. I feel him moving in and taking an interest."

Her small, brave face was ugly with pallor; her hair damp and unlit. Love came up into my throat and choked me. Perhaps she mistook it for pity; she turned her head away from me on the pillow. "And what would you pray for?"

"To be allowed to stay with you. And then, not one mark on your lovely skin."

She frowned and shook her head. "Oh, that doesn't matter. I'm not worried about that." Her face looked sad—darkened by a resigned, grown-up, reflective expression that had not been there before we loved each other. "Poor Dick. It's a bit of a mess, isn't it?"

"It seems to be until I'm with you."

It was not that problems were solved—they simply ceased. Here there was only a present, and no future; and, as it was in the future that problems lay, no problems. The room contained peace as it might have contained the scent of flowers, and the fears I brought with me seemed unreal after a moment or two.

I sat down beside her and took her hand. I could do this now, for her right hand was out of bandages. The first part of her to emerge from the contraptions of reconstruction. It was as it ought to be—the thin wrist straight and the tendons showing close to the skin like the strings of a guitar. For a long time we were quiet and I held her hand, pressing it softly. Her eyes were closed and I thought she was asleep. Then I saw that she had opened her eyes and was looking out along her pillow away from me. A lonely, dark look. I did not know what she was thinking.

"Helen. . . ."

"You won't tell him anything."

So that was all. "Darling, he's a big grown-up man and you have no children."

"*He's* a child."

"Helen, you haven't changed your mind?"

"No!" She turned again and smiled. It was her old smile from the past uncomplicated days when all I wanted from her was an hour's careless physical delight. I pleaded guilty then to Shankar's accusation. It seemed to me that somehow, in some devious, unintended way, I had done this to Helen—laid her down on this bed, broken her straight legs and robbed her forever of her peace of mind. Yet she did not reproach me. She didn't even know. And so would never have to hide the fact of knowing from me, or withhold any accusation, or offer any excessive compensation.

I watched the plane come in from the barrier outside the Transit Lounge, its dark bulk falling lightly down between the rows of lights on the landing strip. A small crowd stood waiting, figures in dhotis and shawls; their rags, molding undernourished bodies, showed them as men and women from the poorer castes, or peasants who had been driven into the capital by disaster in faraway places. I wondered why they stood there, staring out over the airfield, and what that huge machine, falling softly out of the sky, could possibly mean to them.

At first I thought that Fred had missed his plane. The passengers trailed across the runway; those in front had grown to life size and the lights were picking out their tired faces. Then I saw him appear at the top of the gangway and begin to stumble down it—he was carrying so many bags and parcels he had no hands free to hold on with. He made me think of one of those overloaded donkey carts you see in Chandni Chowk, one tiny creature staggering along under the burden of half a dozen stalwart men—women, babies, bundles, beds, sheep.

Halfway to the barrier he saw me and, in a moment of thoughtless pleasure, tried to wave. But the ballast of his load had been disturbed, and a bulky parcel that was hitched on to this arm by a loop of string fell with a clatter to the ground. I began to laugh. Fred always surprised you. He was so much in excess of himself—more than you had ever expected, or been able to remember. I found myself liking him all over again, perhaps because it was so impossible to be afraid of him. Fred would never get around to the big issues in his life. He would always be too busy buying cameras and Cadillacs and getting himself onto planes without paying excess weight.

I stood in the door of the Customs while an official went through his baggage.

"And what is this piece of machinery, sir?"

"It is an electric Mixmaster."

"Is it new?"

"Of course it's new. Would I carry an old Mixmaster around with me on a holiday? It is my personal property."

"Is not for resale?"

"I've *told* you! I live in India. It is my personal property."

"You must pay duty, sir."

"You silly fool! I am a United Nations Expert working for the Government of India. Here is my *laissez-passer*. *Nozing* I bring in is dutiable. You should study your regulations. . . ."

"But you have two portable typewriters."

"Von is for my vife."

"Zos idiots!" he complained, when at last they let him through. "They don't know the regulations. Zey have never seen the *laissez-passer*. Here, will you help me with that?"

I relieved him of one of the portable typewriters, a camera and two bottles of Scotch.

"Where did you get these? Not from the States."

"From Hong Kong. Everything is *very* cheap there. Not as good as Aden but not bad. And to go there it doesn't cost any extra on the ticket."

"So that was why you canceled your trip to Paris."

"I have never been to Hong Kong," he said simply. "It is a

very beautiful place. You ought to go. It is *very* good to see you, Dick." He stopped and smiled, showing me all his big white teeth and the warmth of his trivial, greedy nature. "It is good of you to come and meet me. I can always rely on you. You are the *best* of friends! Where is Elly?"

"She didn't come. I'll tell you later."

Quite contentedly he followed me outside and, while I went for the car, stood busily shooing away porters and taxi drivers.

Driving back into Delhi, I told him about Helen's accident. He took it quite well. No hysteria—but for a while a dignified quiet fell between us. He asked one or two questions. Then he said, "Would they let me see her now?"

It was nearly twelve. "I shouldn't think so. She'd be asleep. Better wait till tomorrow."

Back at the hotel the party was over, and the guests had gone. The lawn was grubby with stamped-out cigarettes, scraps of scarlet paper, a burst balloon tied to a piece of string; but the tables had been cleared away and the chairs stacked up on the veranda.

The light in my room was still burning. It was twelve hours since I had left it—twelve hours since Shankar's letter, the break with Pamela. Now for a moment I allowed myself to remember, and I felt a sharp, short spasm of dread, like the flick of a whip.

"Come with me, Dick. I'm not tired. Are you tired? Come back and we'll talk and have a drink."

So we crossed the darkened lawn to his room. A bush that had been decorated with strings of colored bulbs burned gaily in the dark.

We sat on the beds with all his plunder around us. Fred grumbled because Alisulman hadn't turned on the refrigerator and there was no soda or ice, and only one small bottle of drinking water.

"I'll take mine straight."

We drank half a bottle of Scotch. Once I said, "I ought to go," but he begged me not to, and I made no move. That was around one-thirty. Suddenly he dropped his head in his hands. His shoulders jerked, he made little coughing sounds and I understood he was crying. For a moment I was astonished, and then it seemed quite in order that he should weep. He wasn't ashamed. He cried for a bit in an open, relaxed way—like a child—and then wiped his nose on the back of his hand. I wondered if Helen had to watch much of this sort of thing. I didn't mind—I rather liked him for it. But Helen was Helen McLeish.

"Poor Elly! Zis is awful, Dick. . . . If she can't swim . . ."

"Of course she can swim."

"And play tennis. You've never seen her play tennis. She is an absolutely *terrific* tennis player. She's got a serve like a man. Dick, do you think I ought to take her to Australia? Why are they giving her penicillin? They've mucked her up. I'll bet you they've mucked her up. Zis *bloody* country! Dick, vat do you think?"

He looked up, and the tears were still wet on his cheeks. A dozen times that night I nearly told him. I would have, if I hadn't yet again promised Helen. "Please, not now . . . not yet. . . . It's something that *I* must say. And you have to be able to say it properly, standing up on your own two feet." But in the end I was glad to wait, simply because I wanted his company.

"Have another drink."

"At this rate you won't have much left."

"It doesn't matter. It's good to have you here, Dick. I am *very* grateful for all you have done for Elly. You are a *good* friend. You're the best friend we've got."

When finally I got up to go it was nearly four and the darkness was beginning to lose its density. The red lights still glowed in the bushes; a bird moved. Then the main building came into view. All quiet and dark, except for that one bright window, glaring out at me like a sleepless eye. The sweat broke out on my hands.

I opened the door, and I seemed to be entering a piece of time that I had already lived. I knew the scene before me—the disordered room . . . a chair knocked over, as though some struggle had taken place . . . the sheets pulled from the bed. The smell of terror.

A glass had fallen off the bedside table and the dark mark of water on the carpet had not had time to dry. The bottle had fallen too, but this had been empty.

I went into the bathroom and Pamela was kneeling on the floor, her body folded over the bath, her head and arms drooping down into it. She wore a blue silk dress and a string of pearls, which meant that she must have spent some time at the party, or intended going to it. Perhaps she had crawled in here to try and make herself vomit. The sparrows, nesting in the switch box high on the wall, had dropped pieces of straw on her hair.

Chapter Eighteen

RUPLAL MUST HAVE BEEN LOOKING THROUGH THE WINDOW
when I drove up. He was waiting for me in the outer office.

"I am afraid Sir Malcolm isn't here, sir. He is over at the
Ministry."

"Have you got my ticket?"

"Is here, sir. But I am sorry—the permit for the car still hasn't
come through." He smiled, and his eyes looked directly into
mine. A brief spark of anger lit my mind. But it was an effort
even being angry. I said to myself, You ought to be enjoying
this. You're a keen, perceptive chap. . . . Everything happens
just as you predict. "It is not important, sir. That buyer will
wait."

"How long?"

"I will see it goes through. I will handle everything. I will
write to you."

"And what about the money?"

"It will be paid into your bank account. You will keep this open, sir."

"There's also the small matter of my Agra expenses that the Indian Government hasn't paid me yet."

"I shall see to it, sir. You will get your money."

He held out his hand and I dropped the keys of the car into his pale, salt-colored palm on which the lines of fate were darkly etched. "All the papers are in the front pocket."

He said softly, "Some gentleman in the Ministry is perhaps holding the file and we shall have to see that it goes on its way. We may have to take a little from the proceeds of the sale. . . ."

"I am sure you will do your best."

"Thank you, Mr. Mardellis. You have not changed your mind about the camera? I got a very good sale for Mr. Siegel for the Leica he bought in Hong Kong."

"Mr. Siegel still has his car up his sleeve."

"What was that, sir?"

"Thank you. I'm keeping my camera."

"Well, sir, now I shall say goodbye. . . ."

Inside the main office, Hilton got up from his desk. "I'm sorry, Dick, Sir Malcolm's not here. He's over at the Ministry. He said he'd try and make it to the airport tomorrow."

"Tell him not to worry. I don't care for long goodbyes."

"We sure are sorry to lose you, Dick."

But that was all he was going to be sorry for. And he looked bravely at me with his big, kind, innocent eyes.

Clever girl, I thought. Clever Pamela. That greedy, public gesture—the hand tugging my sleeve, the signal from the other side of the valley: Here I am. . . . Look at me! Never forget me. Small chance! And I saw her achievement in all its total success when Hilton was sorry to see me go but wasn't able to be sorry for what had happened.

It was all too much. For Hilton, Fern, Sir Malcolm, even for Giles. Like a black hole, gaping at their feet. They skirted around it, casting down an occasional nervous glance. And the flowers were for Pamela, not for me. She had proved her case, and it didn't matter that nobody knew what it was. Small wonder it had also been too much for Helen. . . .

I'm sorry, Dick, but I just feel I don't want to see you. It wouldn't do any good, please try to understand. I haven't told Fred anything, and I don't see any point in hurting him, because we can't do anything now. Can we? You must see that. I just wouldn't be able to forget, and I would always be asking myself questions. You just can't go around causing unhappiness, like that, can you? I mean, there's a limit to what you can do. So please don't come and see me, because I haven't stopped loving you, but I feel it's all too much. There's Fred . . . and I feel I just can't deal with it.

Wise girl, wise little Helen. Never have a try at something that might not come off. Love, living daily with this somber presence, might turn nasty on us. Play safe. . . . Don't take risks against incalculable forces. . . .

Outside the heat was like a wall of water into which I pushed my tired body. The day before a scorching wind had scraped the deserts of Rajasthan and flung a load of sand over Delhi. The ugly yellow air looked dark and thick; you felt you could part it with your hand. You tasted grit on your lips. You could look at the sun that was no brighter than a full moon and small and close: livid, like a blind eye.

I crossed the compound, which even the crows had deserted, with the feeling that there was little here to regret. Under the shadow of some trees whose leaves had shriveled into dirty twisted shapes, like pieces of tin foil, half a dozen Sikhs squatted or slept by their motor scooters. They were always here, outside the U.N. Office; they were here today not because they wanted customers but from habit, and because you had to be somewhere. No one moved as I walked up. Those that were awake stared with sad, reddened eyes. Each man had retreated, as far as he could, into the most diminished sense of his existence.

"Take me to the Mayfair Hotel."

"Sahib. . . ." Slowly one tall Sikh got to his feet, but still held back from his life, like a man who stumbles out of his bed at night trying not to waken fully in case he should lose his grip on sleep and be left, lying alone, in the dark, with all his needs and fears parading before him.

Back to the Mayfair for the last time, through roads that were rivers of wind; past houses, trees, tombs degraded by dust; the stupefied cyclists wobbling into the gutters and the slow, hump-backed cattle holding their heads turned against the wind. There were fewer people about and all that anyone seemed to be doing was trying to exist against the weather, as though Delhi were an engine that was still running—it hadn't actually stalled, but it wasn't pushing anything along. You recognized the futility of effort. You simply waited and endured. And I tried to remember something that Pamela had once said about India. It was back in London, after that first dash away:

"There's an atmosphere around the earth, isn't there? Well, we're told there is. Like a warm overcoat, wrapping it up. I'm sure it protects a lot of illusions. Well, I think it's thinner out there. I think you're closer to space. I suppose if I were religious I would say closer to God. No wonder Indians are always talking about Him. You feel His presence. You see Him getting down to things . . . shriveling up deserts, flooding rivers, killing off millions of people. . . . Like a page from Genesis. Because people don't matter to God. It's only to mankind that man matters. So no wonder they haven't any dignity, or any hope. They know that God doesn't care about them; they aren't worth bothering about. There's all the evidence around them, and they can't help holding this view of themselves. I suppose that's what you miss when you go away. You think what a relief to get out of that dreadful country, and you creep back under your thick, soft envelope that cushions you from all the celestial goings on, like a shock absorber. But after a bit it gets boring. And suddenly you want to return. There isn't any shelter there, and nowhere else seems quite real any more. . . ."

A perceptive woman. Not always stupid. Only when it came to dealing with her own life.

Back at the hotel I packed my things. They knew I was going, of course, and one by one they came. The dhobi with the washing and the buttons sewn on; the mallee with a fistful of Soni's red bougainvillaea; Nur; the cook; the tailor; the barber and the small boy responsible for handkerchiefs. Alisulman had no need to come—he was there all the time. And I thought, India has had a lot from me. So why stop at a few rupees? But though they were good servants and I had been fond of them, I hated them then, and I told myself that I would find a fat rich country and fight it out with people who were stronger and crueler than I, people whom you couldn't possibly pity. And maybe in the end I might extract from them a ten-rupee tip and a prayer for my soul.

At about four, Agawalla knocked on the door and handed me a note. It was from Helen. "Please, Dick, come and see me before you go."

Her room seemed cold after mine, and I shivered, wishing I had brought a coat. The machine in the window softly roared and pushed out its clean, chilled air. And this was not India, and therefore should have been an improvement on the world outside, where the pye-dogs barked, the crows cawed and the dust raked the trees. But, to use the language of Pamela's dissertation, God was not looking, and you missed the regard of that casual, pitiless eye.

Helen had been out of hospital now for nearly a week, but it was the first time I had seen her alone. She sat on a chair with her leg in plaster, supported on a low stool. Her arm, also still in plaster, was tied in a sling. She looked thin and sallow, and it was difficult to remember that I had ever thought her beautiful. A rather ordinary, hard, boyish face, and her hair had darkened and needed attention. But Helen's beauty had never centered in any one part of her. She had been all of a piece, total, complete. Like all beauty, I suppose. The harmonious relationship of possibly undistinguished elements. Like a good theatrical production: perfect teamwork between the wrist and the nose, the eye and the fingertips.

"Do sit down, Dick."

Down I sat. "How are you?"

"Not too bad. I got prickly heat and that was a bit grim. I got an itch and made the mistake of scratching under the plaster with a knitting needle. . . . That seemed to start it off. It nearly drove me mad for a night. It was much worse than anything else. But they gave me something and it's better now.

But my God, I'll be glad when I get them off. It's like carrying a ton weight around with you."

"When?"

"Next week."

"Will you write and tell me?"

Her eyes looked directly into mine and I imagined that I saw a stubborn animosity in her expression, though I returned her regard with all the tenderness I could muster. Like a general scraping up the last dregs of his country's manhood—the old, the shortsighted, the boys with bad hearts—to fight the last stages of a losing war. She shook her head. "Fred will write to you. He keeps saying how much he's going to miss you."

"You seem to hate me, Helen."

"You should have told me."

"Told you what, my darling?"

"About Pamela . . . that she tried to kill herself once before."

"Who told you that?"

"Fern. She got it from Hilton. Sir Malcolm told him."

I laughed. "It was a sacred promise. So much for promises."

She said, "I suppose he thought it didn't matter any more."

"I suppose it doesn't. Listen, Helen . . ." I leaned toward her then and I began to talk to her gently and earnestly as though there might still be some hope for us both; as though we might be able to retrieve what had seemed so precious and strong, and might still be able to love each other and live together.

"Listen, my dear. Months ago, when I was in England and before I ever met you, I gave up thinking about all this. Pamela didn't try to kill herself. She was very careful not to pull it off. Sleeping pills again but not enough and they soon came up.

Nasty for her at the time but she got what she wanted. I rushed her out of India."

She said, "My God, the way you dismiss it. I think you just don't want to look at it and accept responsibility. If that's true then why was it different this time?"

"Was it? The doctor said I was only just too late. Half an hour and a stomach pump and she'd still be alive today. I was talking to Fred. I didn't come in till nearly four o'clock and she must have expected me long before then. She found out about you that afternoon—Shankar wrote to her, and I think she simply meant to break us up. But for once I wasn't under the window, holding the net. Too bad. You can go on counting on people just too far. . . ."

"You shouldn't talk about her like that. It's horrible. Haven't you any pity for her?"

"She's used up all my pity."

"You mustn't hate her. That's horrible too."

"Why not? At least it's an honest, straightforward emotion. It should appeal to you. Better than beating my breast and muttering prayers for the rest of my life. Don't you understand what she's done to me? I'm forty-two, and now I haven't got a wife, or a lover or a job. I don't expect I shall look for another wife, but I shall certainly look for a lover and a job. What do I do? What do I say? Is it the first thing I tell an attractive woman or is it the last? Helen, don't let her get away with this. . . ."

And on I went, trying to persuade her. But what with the cold—when it was hot outside—and the noise of the air conditioner stunning my ears, nothing I said seemed to have much meaning. As for hating Pamela, well, you have to invent some feeling to offer the world. I made my choice then and have stuck to it since. It's probably less corrosive than guilt or regret. . . . And when I said "I still love you, Helen," I hoped it was true. It would have seemed wasteful and sad if I had stopped loving her, and I hoped I was only temporarily numb and indifferent. All the time I talked to her I tried to regain my old sense of her uniqueness, my delight in being near her. I tried to imagine myself caressing her. I thought of the moist, silky feel of her skin, and its honey color. And I felt a spark of desire. As I might have felt with any woman. But not as it used to be. Not enough. Then in my mind I pushed her on the bed and fell roughly, eagerly upon her. Only then the scene became funny and ugly because my mind could not remove the plaster from her leg, which stuck up and wobbled heavily about in the air in an uncontrolled way. Added to which, she said, "You're hurting my arm."

I could not get this sour little daydream from my mind, and after I'd said goodbye and had kissed her, and was walking back over the lawn, I asked myself if I had stopped loving her, just for the moment, because now she was incomplete and inadequate, as Pamela had been, only in a different way. But that wouldn't last. She would get better. Or would she? As a matter of fact, she didn't. When they took the plaster off—well, what a mess, according to Fred. So he flew her down to Australia and the whole thing was started over again. But I didn't know that at the time. Even so, there was a doubt in my mind, and I said to myself that I would wait and see, and then I'd know if I could go on loving her.

The thoughts that come to our minds to pull us down in our own estimation. . . . When my father died, I watched by his bed, stupid with grief, and thought, I wish he'd hurry up. I want my dinner. It's as though there is something so attractive about suffering as to invite cruelty, and we cannot even leave ourselves alone, but masturbate for further pain. Yet suffering exalts us and makes us better than ourselves, so perhaps it is as well that these small, salutary voices speak out and remind us of our normal disposition. After all, we shall have to go back to it, and rub along with it again.

So no love—not now, at any rate. Instead I felt only sadness for something lost, and searched bitterly in my mind for someone to blame. Helen herself, Pamela, Shankar. . . .

It was a day for taking count, and a place you are about to leave throws the past back at you. Certain moments return and seem to be the sum of its qualities. Though the lawn was empty, I saw Soni's grandchildren, leaping up to catch their ball, while their dopattas made white undulations in the air; the cattle egret flying overhead in neat formation. And behind the creaking door to the dining room, Ram Chandra saying, "She'll be all right here—Daddy's put air conditioning in the new annex, and he won't allow cats. He says they eat the birds." I went on to my room, thinking of Krishan's death, and what a complexity of motives impel us to the actions we take.

Fred drove me to the airport, and Fred's elder sister, it now turned out, had also committed suicide. The Nazis. . . . He told me about it, and she had had good reason. But Fred was impatient of it. "Zees things happened to a lot of people." Then, in the next breath, "We are going to miss you, Dick. I think it was a great pity you resigned. Was it necessary?"

"My contract was up for renewal, but when Sir Malcolm got around to chasing up my file, it wasn't to be found. It had been mislaid somewhere in the Ministry, which meant that the application had never been made."

"But zis sort of thing is always happening. Zey are such fools. One of our chaps is still working without a contract and some of the Indians haven't been paid for six months."

"Raja—that's my counterpart—told me that Prasad has been trying to get someone else in my place. Another Englishman . . . but he knew him as a child. His father, according to Raja, was a friend of Prasad's. They worked together in the I.C.S."

"Who is this Raja? Has he got it in for you?"

"Possibly. I think he likes me all right, but he hates being pushed around by a European."

"I don't think there's anything in it. He's making it up."

"There's something in it. I saw a letter in a file. And that might have been deliberate too. Prasad is very devious and he doesn't usually let his files drift around. In any case, I don't know what it all amounts to, but I'm not taking any chances."

"I see what you mean. You don't want them to kick you out after that other business. You begin to feel you've had just about enough."

No reticence in Fred. No skirting around the sore spot. And I thought what a long time it had taken me to find out why, against all my reason, I had always liked him. Neither did it seem strange any more that Helen should have married him. They were well suited—both hard, honest, brave and greedy for life. The best of it. The Sunday picnics, and the sunny weather.

The airport was in a state of squalid, noisy confusion as Indian immigrants leaving for England said goodbye to their relations and checked their luggage in. A tall, hysterical official tried to assemble them in line, snatched at tickets, shoved and pushed his way through the thin, soft bodies and dirty bundles. And there they stood: agitated young men, old women and young girls whose childhood was barely behind them, holding sad-eyed babies in their arms.

It was India at its worst—hopeless, dirty, incompetent, confused. I wondered how any of them had managed to get so far, for they were nearly all village people, and had perhaps already traveled many hundreds of miles. I kept looking at the old women and the young mothers, standing dull and inert, as though barely conscious of what was happening to them—submissive, yet curiously obstructive; doing nothing for themselves, yet needing things to be done to them, and diverting the energies of other people. I looked at them, and their courage and the pitiful sadness of their situation passed me by. Instead I saw their gaudy, filthy clothes and clotted hair; the smudged kohl that would injure a baby's eyes; the remains of the last meal that had not been wiped away from a child's mouth and now offered a feast for the flies.

I had had this sort of mood before, when everything in India looked ugly and debased, where there seemed no dignity and no compensating beauty. I had had it in Agra during the seminar when the students, with their hands dripping to the wrist in yellow ghee, had talked about the wisdom of India and the materialism of the declining West. So perhaps it wasn't permanent. Yet it seemed so, as though a chill had fallen upon my emotions; and as it is intolerable to live in India without affection, I said to myself that it was just as well I was going. And doing at last, in the end, what Pamela had always wanted me to do.

Then came Prasad, pushing through the crowd, and Raja with

a marigold garland. The rest of the staff holding back behind. But Fred was the one to push his smile in front of everyone else's and wave me into the Departure Lounge.

Once I was in the plane, India was very soon out of sight, for within a few moments we had climbed up over the blanket of dust that hung like a fog on the land below.

I looked down into red oblivion, thinking that now we were probably passing over Gurgaon; the College might be directly below. Our territory—attacked every day by the forces of reformation. Lean fields that lie disposed in a haphazard arrangement of straggling shapes, like pieces of rag that the Indian scavengers pick from the rubbish dumps to wash and lay out in the sun. The trees low and stunted, their branches, cropped for fodder year after year, having the blunted, deformed look of leper's hands. The earth old and worn, and used to the last of its substance. Picked, scratched, trodden; the skin torn from it; tracks and paths scribbled across it; roads that lead nowhere and start out of nothingness. A wilderness, without beauty or grandeur, and without the solemnity of desolation.

Fred kept his promise—he wrote to me. He was alone in Delhi; Helen had gone back to Australia and was still waiting for the second lot of plaster to be removed. Yes, he had rung up Dr. Batterjee and Shankar Dhas had gone to work in a village in Uttar Pradesh. He was taking no pay, Dr. Batterjee said, but the peasants gave him food when there was any to spare. His wife had gone back to her parents in Madras.

Giles had left Delhi and gone to Lucknow for six months. He was becoming, in Fred's view, more and more strange. Forever in a dhoti and he had given up eating meat, which meant that his dinner parties weren't what they used to be. All that curd and gram. He had taken his dhobi's younger brother to Lucknow with him—a boy of about fifteen and, in Fred's view, very dirty.

With his letter he enclosed a cutting from a Melbourne paper that Helen's mother had sent to him:

Mrs. Frederick Siegel arrived in Melbourne today by plane. She has come from India to receive medical treatment, after having been injured in an accident outside New Delhi when the car in which she was driving ran into and overturned a bullock cart. Mrs. Siegel is the daughter of Mr. and Mrs. Ian McLeish, of Wallaroo, Camperdown.

ABOUT THE AUTHOR

Australian by birth, Geraldine Halls has lived or traveled extensively in New Guinea, India, Thailand, Malaya, Lebanon and Jordan. *The Cats of Benares* is the result of her two-year stay in New Delhi.

After Mrs. Halls left Australia at the age of twenty-one, she worked for a London lawyer, an import agent, and a Soho button manufacturer. Her most interesting job was court stenographer for the Supreme Court at Port Moresby, New Guinea, but these were all, as she says, "preludes to writing."

When not off traveling or buying and selling antiques in London, Mrs. Halls and her husband make their home in The Old Grammar School House near Bath, England.

Format by Katharine Sitterly
Set in Linotype Fairfield
Composed, printed and bound by American Book–Stratford Press, Inc.
HARPER & ROW, PUBLISHERS, INCORPORATED